'My mother *loved* you,' she said shakily.

'No,' he denied. 'She didn't.'

Carolyn's frustration was acute. 'How can you say that?' She had heard her mother quite clearly begging him not to leave her. Her broken voice had torn Carolyn so much that she had run away and hidden, not coming out till she'd heard Vaughan leave.

'Because it's true,' he insisted harshly. 'And your mother knew it too. She wanted sex, that's all, then afterwards she tried calling it love to soothe her conscience.'

Dear Reader

Autumn's here and the nights are drawing in—but when better to settle down with your favourite romances? This month, Mills & Boon have made sure that you won't notice the colder weather—our wide range of love stories are sure to warm the chilliest of hearts! Whether you're wanting a rattling good read, something sweet and magical, or to be carried off to hot, sunny countries—like Australia, Greece or Venezuela—we've got the books to please you.

Enjoy!

The Editor

Miranda Lee is Australian, living near Sydney. Born and raised in the bush, she was boarding-school educated and briefly pursued a classical music career before moving to Sydney and embracing the world of computers. Happily married, with three daughters, she began writing when family commitments kept her at home. She likes to create stories that are believable, modern, fast-paced and sexy. Her interests include reading meaty sagas, doing word puzzles, gambling and going to the movies.

Recent titles by the same author:

ASKING FOR TROUBLE
A DATE WITH DESTINY
A DARING PROPOSITION
KNIGHT TO THE RESCUE

A DAUGHTER'S DILEMMA

BY

MIRANDA LEE

MILLS & BOON LIMITED
ETON HOUSE   18-24 PARADISE ROAD
RICHMOND   SURREY   TW9 1SR

*First published in Great Britain 1992
by Mills & Boon Limited*

© Miranda Lee 1992

*Australian copyright 1992
Philippine copyright 1992
This edition 1992*

ISBN 0 263 77789 8

*Set in Times Roman 11 on 12 pt.
01-9211-50034 C*

Made and printed in Great Britain

CHAPTER ONE

'WOULD all visitors please leave the ship immediately,' came the call along the corridors of the *SS Sea Countess*. 'We will be departing in five minutes.'

'That means me, I guess.' Carolyn sighed and stood up from where she'd been sitting in one of the cabin's luxurious armchairs. She walked across the deep-pile blue carpet and bent to kiss the cheek of the very attractive blonde woman sitting on the side of the bed.

'Have a wonderful honeymoon, Mum,' she said softly. 'You deserve it.'

'Thank you, darling,' Isabel murmured in return, and cast a shy, almost blushing glance at her husband of three hours.

Carolyn smiled with approval as she turned to face her stepfather, who had also risen from his chair. Fifty-two and going bald, Julian Thornton was not a particularly handsome man. But he had a fine build and intelligent grey eyes, as well as a kind and patient nature. He was, in Carolyn's opinion, just the sort of man to make her mother happy.

'As for you, Step-papa,' she said, giving him a kiss also, 'I think you're very naughty depriving me of my mother's company for two whole months. Just as well you're leaving me your lovely car to drive around in or I might have been cross.'

He chuckled. 'Mind you look after it.'

'Carolyn?'

The plaintive note in her mother's voice had her swinging sharply around. 'Yes, Mum?' Hard to keep the worry out of her voice. Surely nothing was going to go wrong now!

'Did . . . did I pack that new hairdryer we had to buy? I just can't remember . . .'

Carolyn tried to ignore the instant jab of dismay. She knew her mother's memory could still be faulty, but she'd been so much better lately and Carolyn had hoped . . .

Suppressing a sigh, she said brightly, 'It's safely packed. We put all your toiletries and accoutrements in here.' Moving briskly, she picked up the smallest of the green leather suitcases lying against the wall and carried it over to place it gently on the bed beside her mother.

Julian stepped up to the foot of the bed. 'Why don't you start unpacking, love,' he suggested to his bride, 'while I see my charming stepdaughter off the ship?'

'All right.' Isabel's voice carried that vaguely resigned compliance Carolyn always hated hearing in her once strong-minded mother.

Biting her bottom lip, she was unsure all of a sudden if her mother was in a fit state to be anybody's wife, even a man as understanding as Julian.

'Come along, Carolyn.' His voice was firm. 'We don't want you sailing with us, do we? Honeymoons are meant for two, not three.'

She glanced up and saw the bittersweet understanding in his face. 'Coming. Bye, Mum.' She gave her mother another parting peck, picked up her bag from the small table near the door and dashed from the room before she did anything stupid like cry.

'Don't worry about her so much,' Julian urged as they walked along the corridor and up the narrow stairway. 'She's tired, that's all. It's been a long day.'

Carolyn shook her head. 'You're so patient with her. So... good.'

'I love her.'

'Yes...' Carolyn swallowed and tried not to think of her mother's words when Julian had first asked her to marry him six months ago.

'But I... I don't *love* him. I mean, I *like* him a lot and he's very kind, but...'

Isabel had turned him down, but Julian was persistent, and Carolyn had to admit that her mother had sincerely warmed to him over the next three months, so much so that, when Julian had asked her again, she had said yes. Nevertheless, Carolyn was sure that their relationship had not yet become a sexual one; a fact which worried her slightly, in the circumstances...

'Carolyn.' Julian stopped beside the gangway and turned to take her hands in his. His grey eyes were steely as they peered down into her own frowning blue ones. 'Let me give you a bit of advice. You're only twenty-four years old, yet you've spent almost ten years being a mother to your own mother. And, while I admire what you've done enormously, it's time you got on with your own life. Your mother's *my* responsibility now. You have to let go of the apron strings, cut them or you'll ruin your own life, as surely as Isabel once almost ruined hers with her exaggerated sense of responsibility.'

Carolyn was taken aback by this last remark till she recalled that Julian believed Isabel's breakdown had been due to the stress of raising an illegitimate child on her own. Carolyn herself trotted out the same excuse whenever one of her friends questioned her mother's odd timidity and vagueness.

Julian had eventually been privy to a more detailed version when he'd started taking Isabel out, and he'd been moved by the story of the innocent young Isabel, falling madly in love with her history professor at college—and vice versa; of her becoming pregnant to this much older professor; of his abandoning his childless and unhappy marriage to live with Isabel and await a divorce and his baby; of his dying of a heart attack before either arrived, leaving the devastated nineteen-year-old mother to cope on her own, which she did very bravely and valiantly, till suddenly, when the child was fourteen, she'd unexpectedly cracked up.

It *was* a touching story. And quite true. Up to a point. Carolyn suspected her mother had by now convinced herself it was the total and real truth. And she'd never contradicted her. How could she? Isabel McKensie had no idea her daughter knew the real reason for her breakdown. And Carolyn had never dared reveal her knowledge for fear of causing a relapse.

'But she's fine now,' Julian was insisting. 'Much better than you give her credit for. The fact is, you've been molly-coddling your mother, Carolyn. Doing far too much, making too many decisions for her.'

Resentment burned inside Carolyn for a moment. 'How can you say that after what you yourself asked me to do earlier in the week? Doesn't that entail my making *more* decisions for her?'

Julian sighed. 'I agree your mother still has some limitations, but my request was more to keep my project a *secret*, rather than because Isabel is incapable of making some simple decisions. I want to present a brand new home to her, fully furnished and decorated, as a surprise when we get home. Perhaps I put it badly when I asked you to oversee the finishing touches for me, to veto anything you thought your mother might not like. If I did, I'm sorry. Look, if you feel it's too much of an imposition on your time——'

'No, no,' Carolyn cut in, overwhelmed by guilt that Julian might think her unwilling to help out when he'd been so good to her and her mother. Impossible to explain that it would take more than a few stern words to make her stop worrying about Isabel. He hadn't been around ten years ago when she'd had her nervous breakdown. He'd never witnessed the sort of woman she'd been beforehand, as compared to afterwards. The difference had been staggering. She shuddered inside at the memory, but kept her face unreadable. No point in worrying Julian at this late stage.

'I'd like to do it. *Really*,' she reassured. Then smiled. 'And you're quite right. I'm going to stop fussing over Mum and leave that up to you.'

Julian beamed. 'Good.' He fished two business cards out of his jacket pocket and pressed them into her right hand. 'Now here's the names, business addresses and phone numbers of the architect and interior decorator I'm using. Both of them are going to be really famous one day, you mark my words.

They have adjoining offices in Wollongong and, though they're not actually partners, there's an unwritten agreement that, if you hire this architect to design a house, you hire this decorator as well. Having met the man, I can understand why. He's a fanatic about his houses. Apparently has nightmares over acquiring some scatter-brained client with lots of money and no taste ruining one of his masterpieces with ghastly décor.

'His words, not mine,' Julian added with a chuckle. 'Anyway, since you have excellent taste, Carolyn, you shouldn't have any trouble with him. But watch yourself. He's in his early thirties and extremely good-looking, but apparently not into marriage. Or so he implied one day when I was talking about the subject. I wouldn't like my step-daughter getting mixed up with an inveterate womaniser. I want her finding herself a husband, not a lover. Why are you looking so surprised? You did tell me you wanted half a dozen children, didn't you?'

'Julian,' she laughed. 'I said *one day* I'd like half a dozen children, not this week, or even this year! And let me assure you that, from the sound of him, your architect is certainly not my type, either for a husband *or* a lover!'

'Believe me, love,' Julian said drily, 'Vaughan's *every* woman's type.'

'Not mine. I can't stand men who...' Carolyn broke off, doing a double take when the architect's Christian name really sank in.

Vaughan?

She resisted succumbing to an irrational burst of panic. It was an unusual name, but not *that* unusual, she reasoned. It couldn't be the same Vaughan. It just couldn't . . . could it?

'Don't worry, you should be pretty safe,' Julian prattled on, 'since I'm fairly sure our architectural Casanova and the interior decorator have a thing going. Miss Powers is very attractive in an offbeat sort of way, and they're *very* intimate in their manner towards each other. But better safe than sorry, so make sure you put that gorgeous hair of yours back up into its usual plait thing when you meet him. And dress like you do for the office. That creation you've got on today is a definite no-no!'

Carolyn glanced down at the scarlet crêpe sheath she'd worn for her mother's wedding. Isabel's choice, not hers. As was her wearing her waist-length honey-blonde hair loose.

'Whatever you say, Julian,' she agreed lightly, but her right hand was tightly closed around the business cards lying within her palm. One quick look and she'd be absolutely sure if Julian's Vaughan and *her* Vaughan were one and the same. One quick look . . .

Why, then, wasn't she taking it?

The answer was quite simple. She already knew the ghastly truth.

The picture Julian was painting of this particular Vaughan coincided too well with the picture that was burnt indelibly in her brain. As well as the two men's both being architects, there could be no mistaking the other similarities. The man's age . . . his magnetic sex appeal . . . his self-centred ambition . . . his ego . . .

Carolyn felt all the blood begin to drain from her face.

'Go looking like the secretary in the Beverly Hillbillies,' Julian laughed, not noticing her pallor under her make-up. 'That should do it! Now, you're to ring Vaughan's office to make an appointment to see both parties this coming weekend. They're already *au fait* with your role in this and my wish to keep the house a secret from Isabel. Here's my petrol card as well . . .'

He extended a plastic card from his wallet and handed it over as well. 'That car of mine is a real gas-guzzler, so don't hesitate to use this to fill up. No, don't argue with me. I insist. I'm the one who's asking you to travel over fifty miles down the south coast every other weekend, so I'm the one who should provide the transport, free of charge. It's all tax deductible anyway.' He smiled.

How she managed to smile back remained a mystery to Carolyn. This wasn't happening. This couldn't be happening. God, what was she going to do?

Nothing at the moment, she realised as Julian bent to kiss her goodbye. 'Thanks again,' he said. 'Keep well, and don't worry about your mother.'

Don't worry about your mother . . .

Carolyn was still shaking her head over the irony of those words as she watched the liner pull away from the pier and slowly make its way across Sydney harbour towards the bridge. If the surname on the architect's card in her hand was the surname she believed it was, she would do nothing *else* but worry about her mother over the next two months.

Slowly, as though her palm contained a deadly funnel-web spider, Carolyn lifted her hand and opened the fingers. The card in question was the first on the pile. Plain white, with black lettering. Its wording was simple.

Vaughan Slater - Architect.
Nothing too large or too small.

Carolyn didn't know whether to laugh, or cry, or be sick.

In the end, she was simply furious at fate, and stuffed the card in her bag with the others before she ripped it into a million pieces.

'Vaughan Slater,' she muttered aloud through gritted teeth.

Vaughan Slater, who ten years ago was a student in architecture at Sydney University and living in their home as a boarder during his final year.

Vaughan Slater, nine years younger than her mother back then. Only twenty-four to her thirty-three. But old enough to take advantage of a woman alone. Old enough to seduce her, sleep with her, make her fall in love with him, then tell her it was 'only sex' to her face and just walk away.

Vaughan Slater... the single and sole reason for her mother's breakdown all those years ago.

CHAPTER TWO

CAROLYN glanced at her watch as she drove into Wollongong. Nearly ten-forty. Her appointment with Vaughan wasn't till eleven, with the interior decorator following at eleven-thirty. Much as she wasn't looking forward to meeting Vaughan again, she didn't want to be late.

She hadn't actually spoken to the man himself when she'd rung his office earlier in the week, his secretary making both appointments for her for this Saturday morning. So he had no idea of her true identity. The secretary had started calling her Miss Thornton straight away and Carolyn hadn't corrected her mistake. At the time, she wasn't sure why she'd kept her real name a secret, but she suspected one never gave an enemy any advantage in advance.

For he *was* an enemy, she accepted, a bitter taste coming into her mouth. An enemy to her mother's future happiness. Carolyn knew that, when Julian presented his new bride with a designer-built and fully furnished home, Isabel was sure to want to meet and thank the people responsible.

Carolyn grimaced as she tried to picture how her mother would react to meeting Vaughan again, to having the man she'd loved so obsessively come back into her life. She wouldn't be able to cope. Of that Carolyn was sure.

I can't let them meet again, she vowed fiercely. I won't!

The street that housed Vaughan's office appeared on the right with Carolyn negotiating the turn across the on-coming traffic with great care. The last thing she wanted was to prang Julian's beautiful blue BMW. Actually, she'd have driven her old bomb of a Datsun if she'd thought it would make the trip. As it was, she sighed with relief once she slid the car safely into a parking spot and turned off the engine.

Her watch showed ten forty-four by the time she alighted and locked the car then set out to find number sixteen. But as she walked swiftly along, the imminence of her encounter with Vaughan began sending a thousand nervous flutterings into her stomach, and her earlier steely resolve threatened to desert her.

Carolyn ground to a halt and scooped in several steadying breaths. Truly, she just had to get a grip on herself or risk making a hash of this meeting. A cool head was required. Vaughan was a successful and professional man now, who wasn't going to like being put on the spot, or having old skeletons dragged out of the closet. He certainly wasn't going to appreciate being told he had to avoid meeting a client's wife, even if it meant lying to that client. For that was the only way Carolyn could think of to tackle the situation, by virtually throwing herself on his mercy. If the devil had any, that was!

At least she had a few weapons to fall back on to persuade Vaughan into compliance. No doubt Julian hadn't paid him the full balance of his fat architectural fee for designing the house as yet. The Vaughan Slater she knew and despised would not do anything to make waves and lose out on *that*, Carolyn thought with bitter cynicism.

Money meant a great deal to him. Hadn't she subsequently found out, when she'd checked the bankbooks after her mother's breakdown, that he had not paid one cent in board for the last few months he'd stayed in their home? One didn't have to have too much of an imagination to work out what happened. Once he'd secured his landlady's love through pretending a return of affection with some very convincing words and lovemaking, he'd simply not paid any more.

Thinking about this little snippet of damning evidence made Carolyn even more determined not to take any nonsense from this man. He'd do what she asked or reap the rewards of his folly. Julian loved Isabel to distraction. He was also a very wealthy and influential businessman around Sydney and the south coast, being the owner and managing director of a large construction company that built shopping centres. Carolyn didn't think he'd take too kindly to finding out the unabridged and disgusting truth of the way his womanising architect had once treated his wife.

Carolyn's blue eyes darkened with fury and her teeth clenched down hard in her jaw.

Amazing, she thought. She'd had no idea she possessed such a capacity for hatred and revenge. People always described her as being mild-tempered. She certainly didn't feel mild-tempered whenever she thought of a certain individual.

Steeling herself again, she walked more confidently along the pavement, looking for the dreaded address.

It wasn't far, a modern three-storeyed steel and glass building with huge bluish windows facing the ocean, the kind of glass that one could look out of but couldn't see into from outside.

Carolyn took one last steadying breath and pushed through the revolving glass doors into a grey marbled air-conditioned lobby. There was no reception desk, only a huge noticeboard on the wall which told her her quarry resided on the top floor. So did the interior decorator—Madeline Powers. Suites Three and Four respectively. A flight of stairs and two lifts serviced these upper floors.

Carolyn chose the stairs. She still had a few minutes to kill.

Would he recognise her straight away? she wondered as she made her way slowly up the carpeted staircase.

It was possible, her basic features not having changed much over the years. She still wore her straight hair in a single plait most of the time, though nowadays she wound it round the top of her head in a coronet. She also never wore make-up during the day, her natural peaches and cream complexion and thickly lashed blue eyes holding up quite well *au naturel*.

He wouldn't have changed much, she fancied. Men didn't from their mid-twenties to early thirties. Unless, of course, they put on weight or went bald, which she doubted he had from Julian's description.

Carolyn still had a rather vivid mental picture of Vaughan at twenty-four, despite the intervening years. A strong angular face with straight brown brows and deeply set brown eyes; thick, wavy chestnut hair that always seemed to need a cut; a sensual-looking mouth that rarely smiled; and a body that had brought her girlfriends running from miles around, especially when he mowed the lawn with his shirt off.

Carolyn cringed as she recalled some of the comments her classmates had made about his various physical attributes. Maybe she'd been a bit of a prude back then, for she certainly hadn't shared her friends' preoccupation with sex. Admittedly, she'd been a young fourteen at the time, but even now she wasn't impressed by the type of man who flaunted his sexual equipment in overtight clothes, any more than she liked girls who went round half-naked!

Maybe I'm *still* a prude, came the agitated thought. Twenty-four-year-old virgins aren't exactly thick on the ground these days.

Carolyn became uncomfortably aware that her forehead had broken out in a fine layer of sweat. Extracting a tissue from her bag, she dabbed herself dry, conceding that perhaps she was dressed a little too warmly for a hot February day, Julian's warning over her dress having induced her to wear a grey suit that the girls at work labelled the most effective in her 'anti Maurice Jenkins' armoury.

Carolyn smiled ruefully at the accuracy of this description, since the suit was rather shapeless with a blazer-style jacket and a pleated skirt. It certainly hadn't caught the eye of the aforementioned Dr Jenkins, an obstetrician at the private hospital where Carolyn worked, who had steadily seduced every attractive nurse in the place and was currently directing his attention towards the administration staff.

Maurice Jenkins might be a handsome and successful man, but no male was welcome in her life on a 'just sex' basis; never had been and never would be. Which perhaps was why she hadn't had a steady boyfriend as yet. All men seemed to want from a girl these days was sex. Carolyn resented being...

Good grief, where was her mind taking her? This was hardly the moment to start analysing and defending her attitude to men and sex. She was here on a mission concerning her *mother's* future, not her own.

Carolyn finally reached the top of the stairs where an arrow indicated that Suites Three and Four were along the corridor to the right. Gathering herself, she made sure all the buttons on her jacket were done up before making a right-hand turn on the motley brown carpet.

No sooner had she begun walking down the corridor than a door opened a little way along and a tall, broad-shouldered man strode out, swiftly followed by a flashy-looking brunette dressed in a purple trouser-suit.

'But Vaughan, darling,' she was saying, the name bringing Carolyn up with a jerk. Her startled gaze snapped back to the man, who had spun round to be half-turned away from her.

This was the present-day Vaughan Slater? she gaped. This conservative male person with short back and sides and dressed in a crisp pale blue shirt and casual cream tailored trousers? Admittedly, the back of the shirt collar was turned up as though he'd dressed in a hurry, but on the whole he presented a smart, well-groomed image—a far cry from the bronzed, shirtless, bejeaned figure all her girl-friends had drooled over.

Quite without warning, he twisted to glance over his shoulder at her, eyes narrowing, straight dark brows bunching into a frown.

Carolyn steadfastly ignored the way her heart started pounding. Nerves, she realised, and steeled herself for the fray. At least his almost sullen expression was still the same, she grumbled to herself. Pity he'd cut his hair, though. She would have liked to have more to remind her of the Vaughan of old. But there wasn't much evidence of those once wild chestnut waves in the dark, damp-looking, semi-spiked hair that covered the top of his head.

When he kept on staring at her, a breathless anticipation seized Carolyn. Any second now the penny was sure to drop.

But it didn't! Oh, yes, there was a split second when something hovered behind his eyes, but he lost it, and, shrugging, returned his attention to the brunette.

'Anthea,' he said in a deep male voice, 'I can't talk to you now. I have a client due at eleven . . .'

The brunette tossed a glance of her own down the corridor to where Carolyn had frozen on the spot.

'Look, I'll ring you later and let you know,' he went on impatiently.

'And turn me down, no doubt,' the brunette huffed. 'Truly, Vaughan, what *have* you got against parties? Oh, please do say you'll come this time, darling. I'm only putting it on for you. I want to show you off to my friends.'

Carolyn actually saw him shudder. 'Good God, I'm not one of your prized poodles, you know. As for the crowd you mix with being *your* friends— huh! They're more your husband's friends than yours, dear heart,' he finished with a snort. 'Especially the women.'

The woman laughed and made the tellingly intimate gesture of straightening his collar. 'True,' she murmured, and traced a fingernail along his jawline. 'That's just the point. I want all those bitches to see what I've finally snared for myself. They'll be as jealous as sin.'

Carolyn's whole insides contracted with distaste. He hadn't changed. Not one iota. She'd had a fleeting worry the other night that she might have misjudged the situation with her mother. But no...he was going along in his usual despicable fashion. At least now he wasn't seducing lonely, vulnerable single women. He'd moved on to tacky, wealthy married ones. Though if what Julian suspected was right, this Anthea was not the only string to his sexual bow. There was the interior decorator as well. My, but he was a busy boy!

Her lips curled with contempt as she walked right up to them.

'Mr Slater?' she said archly.

His companion looked irritated at being interrupted. Vaughan turned and stared hard at her again, as though still trying to place her. Once more his memory failed him, shown by a flicker of frustration in his expressive brown eyes.

You'll know who I am soon enough, she thought tartly. Then you'll wish you didn't, you immoral bastard!

'Yes?' he said, a faint frown remaining on his undeniably handsome face.

Carolyn was rather startled at finding herself admitting to this. When she was fourteen, she'd never thought him all that handsome. Attractive, yes. But only in a sexily brooding fashion. Either his facial features had matured favourably in the intervening years, or she'd changed her ideas on what was handsome and what was not. She certainly couldn't find any fault in the way his face was assembled, from his wide clear forehead to his strong straight nose to his classically chiselled jawline. His eyes, she conceded, had always held some appeal, but she was perturbed to find her own locking with those rich brown depths for an uncomfortable period of time.

'I'm Julian Thornton's stepdaughter,' she said somewhat stiffly at last. 'I believe you're expecting me?'

He glanced at his watch which showed right on eleven. As he raised his eyes, Carolyn was subjected to a fleeting but decidedly dismissive sexual scrutiny.

'I'll be with you in a few minutes, Miss Thornton,' he said coolly. 'If you'll just go into my office, my secretary will show you a seat.'

Piqued at being made to wait—or was it because he'd found her not worth a second glance?— Carolyn swept on into Suite Three, her face burning. What on earth was wrong with her? Fancy even caring what he thought of her looks! So he was drop-dead handsome. So what? Handsome is as handsome does, she believed. And she knew *exactly* what Mr Casanova Slater did with the women in his life!

The middle-aged lady behind the reception desk looked up with a ready smile. 'Miss Thornton?'

Carolyn's returning smile felt decidedly false within her flushed cheeks. 'Mr Slater said for you to show me into his office. He'll be joining me shortly. He's just saying goodbye to his—er...' She bit her bottom lip, aware she'd been about to make an uncharacteristically catty remark. 'I didn't quite catch the lady's name,' she finished lamely.

'Mrs Maxwell,' the secretary supplied, and stood up. 'She's one of Mr Slater's best clients.'

Oh, how typical, Carolyn thought, and almost laughed. Well he certainly hadn't lost his touch when it came to seducing the *right* women, the ones who were to his financial advantage.

'Are you *sure* Mr Slater said you were to wait for him in his office, Miss Thornton?' the secretary enquired on a puzzled note.

Carolyn blinked her confusion. 'Yes...I...I'm *certain* that's what he said.'

The woman shrugged resignedly. 'Very well, but I must warn you not to touch anything. Oh, and—er—don't mind the mess. Mr Slater was working most of the night on a new project, and when he does that he's inclined to be...um...untidy. He went home a short while back to shower and change and was about to clear everything away in readiness for your visit when Mrs Maxwell arrived unexpectedly. He hasn't had time since.'

I can imagine, came the caustic thought. 'I don't mind a little mess,' Carolyn lied.

Even so, when she was shown into the room, she was shocked into a wide-eyed silence. Papers and sketches and plans covered every available surface, which included several desks and cabinets, not to mention every chair and sections of the floor. One of the corners contained a pile of screwed-up paper. Several empty coffee-mugs seemed to be being used as paperweights at strategic points. The litter from a couple of visits to McDonald's was sitting on an old plastic chair beside the main desk.

The secretary picked this latter up with a disapproving 'tch-tch'. 'Truly, it's a wonder that man doesn't have a weight problem,' she muttered. 'The rubbish he stuffs into himself. You'll have to sit here,' she added with an apologetic grimace, and indicated the now empty plastic chair. 'I don't dare touch any of the rest of it. It might cost me my job if I disturb any of Mr Slater's papers.'

Carolyn, who was the neatest, most organised person both at work and at home, could only sink down into the seat and stare at the shambles in bewilderment. The whole place was made to look worse by the clarity and peace of the panoramic view provided by the wall of glass beyond it. Carolyn stared out at the crystalline blue waters of the Pacific Ocean and the perfection of clean white sands, then back at the littered room, shaking her head in amazement.

'But how can he work in this mess?' she asked.

'Very well indeed,' the man himself ground out, making Carolyn flinch as he came in with aggressive strides. 'Why on earth did you bring her in here, Nora? You know I——'

'It's *my* fault,' Carolyn broke in hurriedly, bringing a look of relief to the secretary's instantly stricken face. 'You told me to wait for you in your office and I naturally assumed...'

Her voice died when she noticed he was frowning at her again. After several excruciating seconds, he tore his eyes away and threw his secretary a withering look. '*Never* bring anyone in here unless I'm present, Nora,' he snapped. 'Do I make myself clear?'

The secretary practically quivered in her sensible brogues. 'Yes, Mr Slater,' she said, and fled.

'She's fairly new,' he muttered once she'd closed the door. 'Doesn't know the ropes yet.'

Maybe you should give her one to hang herself with, Carolyn thought crossly, infuriated at the way he'd spoken to the poor woman.

He strode round behind his desk and began shuffling the papers on it into a still untidy bundle. All of a sudden he sighed and looked up, shocking Carolyn when an amazingly engaging smile spread across his previously scowling face.

'I guess I was a bit rough on the old dear,' he said with a rueful chuckle. 'Do you think she'll quit on me?'

Not if you smile at her like that every once in a while, came her treacherous and shattering thought.

Carolyn's stomach fluttered then tightened, the implications of which did not escape her. 'I have no idea,' she said stiffly, wanting to look away but unable to.

I'm physically attracted to him, she was thinking with appalled horror.

He nodded, his smile turning wry. 'It's just that on one occasion I had a whole month's work ruined by having something spilt on them. Then a previous secretary of mine let a slick smooth-talking salesman type come in to supposedly wait for me, and while he was in here he photographed a whole heap of my house plans and sold them to some very unscrupulous builders.'

'How very upsetting for you,' Carolyn said with a betraying lack of sympathy.

His quite beautiful brown eyes narrowed perceptibly. 'Tell me, Miss Thornton, I get the feeling we've met before. Am I right?'

Carolyn swallowed the enormous lump that was filling her throat.

'Yes,' she said simply, merely because she was incapable of elaboration at that point in time.

'I thought so.' A brief look of satisfaction passed over his face before it turned into a frown. 'Yet the name Thornton means nothing to me. Your father is the first Thornton I've ever met.'

'Stepfather,' she corrected in a strangled tone. 'My name isn't Thornton.'

'Aah, yes... My mistake. But... wasn't Miss *Thornton* the name you gave Nora?'

Puzzled brown eyes narrowed some more and a small shiver ran through her. He walked round the desk and cleared a spot on the edge, perching there barely an arm's length from her. He put an elbow on one knee and leant forward, chin resting in his hand. It brought his face much closer to hers. Suddenly, her eyes were on his mouth and she began thinking how sensually full his bottom lip was.

'Care to explain the reason for the deception?' he probed softly.

Her eyes must have revealed something of her inner turmoil, or perhaps it was the way she physically shrank back into the chair to remove herself from his suffocating nearness, for he stiffened and straightened, his expression worried now. 'I'm not going to like your reason, am I?' he announced with dry intuition.

'No,' she rasped.

'Out with it, then,' he said brusquely, sliding off the desk and returning to stand behind his desk, hands on hips. 'I like to take bad medicine in quick doses.'

'Very well.' She had herself under control again now, disgust at her sexual response to this man finding inner steel with a vengeance. How could you? her conscience kept screaming at her. How *could* you?

'My name's McKensie,' she said with an icily controlled fury. 'Carolyn McKensie... If you don't remember me, I'm sure you must remember my mother. Her name's Isabel McKensie, though it changed last Thursday to Isabel Thornton.'

CHAPTER THREE

IF SHE'D been expecting him to blush guiltily, or show shock, she would have been bitterly disappointed. As it was, Carolyn *did* expect a little more reaction than she got.

He merely kept looking at her for a few seconds, that faint frown back on his face. Then he bent to scoop his chair under his knees, sinking into it with a sigh. 'Awkward,' he murmured, rubbing his chin thoughtfully.

'Is that all you've got to say?' she flung at him in simmering outrage. 'Just *awkward*?'

He eyed her closely till she shifted uncomfortably in her chair. 'What else would you like me to say?'

She dragged in a deep breath and took the plunge. 'I'm not going to beat around the bush, Vaughan. I *know* what really happened between you and Mum. Not that Mum told me. She never speaks of that time in her life any more. But I saw you both...together...the night before you left. I came home early from ballet rehearsals because there was a bomb scare in the hall. You were...'

She gulped, then raced on, her voice a few decibels higher. 'Well, let's just say neither of you noticed me standing in the doorway of the living room. I left again in a hurry. I also overheard part of the argument you had with Mum the next day after she told you she loved you. No, please don't

28

say anything. I don't wish to discuss the past or to apportion blame or pass judgements. But you must appreciate that I don't want you seeing my mother again, under any circumstances. I want your word that when Julian and my mother come back from their trip in two months' time you'll avoid meeting her at all costs, because I——'

'Oh don't be so bloody melodramatic!' he cut in forcibly. 'This all happened ten *years* ago, for God's sake. An *eternity*! I'm not going to do any such thing as run and hide from Isabel. OK, so I agree our first meeting might be a little embarrassing, but let's not make a mountain out of a molehill.'

Carolyn could only sit and stare at him.

'Why are you looking at me like that?' he demanded impatiently. 'Is there something here I don't know?'

It finally dawned on her that he just didn't feel any guilt at all over her mother. To him, having love affairs was as natural as breathing. Women came and women went. Clearly he never lost a night's sleep over their demise and he expected them to be the same. Vaughan Slater was on a different moral wavelength from her and nothing would ever change that.

But she had to try to make him see her point of view.

'My mother *loved* you,' she said shakily.

'No,' he denied. 'She didn't.'

Carolyn's frustration was acute. 'How can you say that?' Good God, she had heard her mother quite clearly, telling the wretched creature, begging him not to leave her. Her broken voice had torn Carolyn so much that she had run away and hidden

in her bedroom, not coming out till she'd heard
Vaughan leave a couple of hours later.

'Because it's true,' he insisted harshly. 'And your
mother damn well knew it too. She wanted sex,
that's all, then afterwards she tried calling it love
to soothe her conscience.'

'*Her* conscience!'

'That's right. If you think it was me who was
doing the seducing, then think again, my girl.'

'But...but...' Her confusion was total, her shock
shattering. For there was an undeniable ring of
truth in this callous man's hard voice. Besides, why
should he lie? What reason could he have?

Her distressed eyes dropped to the floor and she
shook her head in anguished bewilderment.

'Carolyn, look at me...'

His voice was so unexpectedly gentle that she was
impelled to look up, only to be lanced by a look of
such incredible warmth and apology that she was
stunned. His regretful gaze washed over her, totally
defusing her anger, making her melt inside.

Panic clutched at her stomach. Dear heaven...she
would have to be very very careful with this man.

'I shouldn't have said that quite so bluntly,' he
murmured. 'I'm sorry. Look, your mother was a
lovely woman. *Very* lovely. But very, very lonely.
She needed a man in her life. I was just...there.
I never led her on and I never told her I loved her.
She came to *me*, not the other way around. I don't
blame her and neither should you.'

'I *don't*,' she bit out, shaking inside with indig-
nation. 'Look, I don't know if you're telling the
truth or not about who started what, but you're

lying about not having told Mum you loved her. You *did*. I know that for a fact!'

An electric silence descended on the pair of them with her vehement accusation.

'Then I suggest you check your facts,' he said at last in a low, tightly controlled voice. 'If your mother thought I loved her then it was all in her mind, certainly not because of anything I ever said or did. I would quite willingly swear to that on a stack of bibles!'

Her belief in his treachery wavered under this intense denial. Could he be telling the truth about everything? Had her mother's mind already been affected so much that she'd started imagining he'd said words he hadn't? Carolyn supposed it was possible, given the obsessive nature of her mother's feelings for him.

What *was* the truth? she agonised. He claimed Isabel had been lonely...frustrated...

Carolyn supposed that could have been true. For not in all her growing-up years could she recall her mother going out with a man, or having a man in the house. Isabel had always insisted she'd loved Carolyn's father far too much to ever look at another man. As an innocent child, she had accepted this as a wonderful, romantic concept. Now she could see that such loyalty to a dead man must have been hard on a normal healthy woman in the prime of her life.

But none of that changed the fact that her mother had *believed* Vaughan loved her. No one could doubt that if they'd heard her piteous ravings that day. Besides, it was the only reason that made sense of her breakdown. Isabel had been a strong woman, not a dreamer. So *why* had she believed Vaughan loved her if he'd not actually said so?

Carolyn lifted her pale face to stare at him across the desk. The answers had to lie in this man's sexual power and prowess, in his ability to bewitch women and make them mad for him without having to say the words women always wanted to hear.

I love you . . . I love you . . .

The words seemed to ring aloud inside her head again and again and she wanted to clasp her hands over her ears to stop them. As it was, the blood drained from her face as an appalling thought hit her. What if he bewitches me too? What if . . . ?

'You look upset, Carolyn,' he said abruptly, and stood up. 'I'll get Nora to make us both a cup of coffee. Then we'll try to sort this out, come to a compromise that will ease your mind. Perhaps I could telephone your mother when she gets back and——'

'Don't you dare!' she burst out, so savagely that he sat down again, looking stunned.

'You . . . you don't understand,' she added, her voice trembling. Oh this was dreadful. Simply dreadful. She had to get a hold of herself.

'Then perhaps you could enlighten me?' he asked quietly.

'I . . . my mother had a nervous breakdown,' she blurted out. 'The day after you left. Her doctor put her in a hospital for a while. Even when she was allowed out, she took a long time to get better. In fact she's still very . . . fragile.'

Vaughan was looking at her as though she were mad. 'Isabel had a nervous breakdown? *Isabel*? Over *me*?'

'Yes.'

'I don't believe it!'

'It's only too true,' she insisted wretchedly, thinking that she would never forget the pitiful scene she'd encountered soon after Vaughan had left. She'd found her mother curled up in a little ball in a corner of the kitchen, talking to herself, totally unaware of Carolyn's presence.

'He swore he really loved me,' she'd raved over and over. 'Why else did he think I started sleeping with him, even though I knew it was wrong? And what did he do in the end? Told me it was only sex, said he was leaving me. All lies... Nothing but lies... Lies, lies, lies! I can't bear it any more... I can't!'

And she hadn't been able to bear it. The rantings had finally dissolved into tears and she hadn't been able to stop. Uncontrollable hysterical tears. Racking her. Tearing her apart.

In tears herself, Carolyn had rung their local doctor and the nightmare had begun...

Remembering what had really happened brought fresh doubts. Could Vaughan be still lying? Had he, in fact, both seduced Isabel *and* told her he loved her? She only had his word for it that he hadn't. Carolyn lifted her eyes to those seemingly sincere brown ones and didn't know what to believe any more.

'Perhaps some of it was in her mind,' she conceded in confusion. 'The bit about you having said you loved her. But she believed it enough to crack up over your leaving. Ten years ago or not, I don't intend risking my mother's mental health by your seeing her again. If you've got a shred of decency in you, Vaughan, you'll keep as far away from her as you can.'

He said nothing for several seconds, his face undeniably disturbed. 'I can't say I appreciate the way you put that, but in the circumstances I suppose I'll have to do as you ask.'

He rubbed his chin again in what was obviously an habitual expression of agitation. 'Hell . . . it's all so damned incredible. I still can't take it in. Isabel was always such a together lady. I admit I was taken aback when she started saying she loved me that day. But I talked to her about it and she seemed to agree with me in the end that it was only a physical thing that had unfortunately got out of hand. I thought it was a mutual decision that I leave straight away. I would have been leaving in another week or so anyway, since I'd finished my exams the day before. She must have been only pretending she didn't mind. She *was* rather unusually quiet . . .

'Poor Isabel,' he sighed, grimacing before looking up again. 'And poor little Carolyn . . . I know you didn't have any family in Sydney. How on earth did you cope?'

'I managed,' she said, her susceptibility to this unexpectedly sympathetic Vaughan making her curt. But he'd certainly been very convincing with his version of the story.

'But where did you go? What did you do?'

'After Mum came out of hospital a cousin let us live with him for a couple of years on his farm in the country. But he couldn't let us stay forever. Things were very bad for farmers at the time, what with the recent floods and the economy. When his wife became pregnant with her fourth child, I took

Mum back to Sydney to live. She had an invalid pension and I left school and got a job.'

'But you must have been only about sixteen!' He seemed appalled. 'Good God, Carolyn, you were always such a bright kid. You should have finished school and gone to college! Damn it, if only I'd known. Perhaps I could have done *something*.'

What? she thought bitterly. Paid us back the board money?

'We managed perfectly well, thank you,' she retorted, not wanting this man's pity, or anything else! 'I have a very good job now. I've never regretted not going to college. I'm happy and Mum's happy. I just want to make sure things stay that way.'

She glared at him, but down deep in her heart Carolyn suspected that already her own happiness was on the line. She'd been attracted to quite a few men since growing up. But never had she experienced the sort of inner upheaval she felt whenever Vaughan looked at her.

'Have you considered the possibility,' he said finally, 'that Julian might mention my name to Isabel?'

Carolyn dragged in a deep steadying breath. 'He won't mention you to her till after he's presented her with the house, since he wants it to be a surprise. I should be able to get him alone before then and make up some plausible story about you without going into too much detail. You leave that up to me.'

'Very well, though I don't really agree with you. I think the open and honest approach would be best. Your mother must be well and truly over me by now. After all, she's just married another man.'

But she doesn't love him, Carolyn was reminded. If she sees you again, especially as you are today, so handsome, so successful, so damned sexy... all those old futile desires could be revived. It wouldn't take much to tip the more fragile Isabel over the edge again.

'Please allow me to be the best judge of that,' Carolyn said stiffly.

'Very well,' he replied just as stiffly. 'But that particular problem's two months away. Right now I would like to address a more immediate problem. Julian's house.'

'Oh? Is there a problem with it?'

His eyes narrowed as they travelled over her tensely held body. 'Not unless you give me one. Are you going to?'

He kept watching her almost warily and Carolyn wondered what he was getting at. 'I have no idea,' she hedged. 'I haven't seen it yet.'

'I doubt that'll make a damned bit of difference,' he muttered, confusing her all the more. 'Well? When do you want to see it? This afternoon some time?'

A quick glance at her watch showed eleven twenty-eight. 'I have a half-hour appointment to see Miss Powers at eleven-thirty,' she stated, hoping a businesslike manner would hide the emotional distress this encounter had evoked. 'Perhaps the three of us could go and see the house together after that. Do you think that would be possible?'

Vaughan shook his head. 'Unfortunately Maddie has another client at twelve whom she can't put off and who'll take at least an hour. I tell you what. After you've finished with her I'll take you to lunch, then the three of us can meet up at the house around two.'

Carolyn only just managed to control the look of horror that threatened to spread across her face. She didn't want to do anything as intimate as have lunch with him. Bad enough to have to put up with the occasional conducted tour around the house over the next couple of months.

'Thank you for the offer,' she said crisply, 'but I'm afraid I'm not very hungry.' She stood up. 'Perhaps you could drop me off at the house and I can have a look around by myself while you go and have lunch.'

This suggestion brought a sharp glance. Vaughan stood up slowly, his eyes remaining hard as he came round the desk to join her. 'I couldn't do that. The place is a bit rough and you might hurt yourself. Look, there's no point in your avoiding my company, Carolyn. It's rather silly and schoolgirlish.'

Her blue eyes flashed with automatic pique. If there was anything she wasn't, it was silly and schoolgirlish. My God, she'd had to assume the mantle of adulthood from a very early age, by-passing the life of a normal teenager, never having the sort of mindless fun adolescent girls indulged in. And all because of this man and his compulsion to bed every woman who came across his path. Her mother... Madeline Powers... Anthea Maxwell... And how many countless others?

Just as well that she had unwittingly taken Justin's advice and made herself as unattractive as possible, otherwise he might even now be attempting to seduce *her*! Given this unwanted though undeniable sexual attraction she was feeling for him, who knew what disaster might have come of it?

'I wasn't avoiding your company,' she lied frostily.

His sardonic smile showed he didn't believe her for a moment. 'In that case you can come with me and nurse a drink while I eat.'

Before she could stop him he took her elbow and began to usher her from the room. 'You can tell me all about what you're doing these days. Oddly enough, I've often thought of you over the years,' came the wry remark. 'Hard to dismiss the pretty blue-eyed little thing who used to glare at me with such obvious disapproval. Something which hasn't changed much, has it?' he added drily when she pulled away from him at the door. 'You still think I'm some kind of ogre.'

'Not at all,' she returned with admirable coolness. 'I don't think of you as anything any more. You're just my stepfather's architect.'

'Is that so?' His gaze turned hard as it locked with hers. 'And how should I think of you, Carolyn? As my client's stepdaughter, here to help finish his house to everyone's satisfaction? Or as a female harbouring an irrational grudge against me and who might be thinking of sabotaging my work out of revenge?'

She gasped with true shock.

'I think any suspicion on my part is well warranted,' he went on coldly. 'After all, you did give a false name to my secretary, then you wangled your way into my office. If I hadn't come in when I did, you would have been left alone with my plans to do God knows what to them. And just now, you seemed eager to be left alone at the house. I wonder what might have been missing or damaged when I returned?'

Her eyes widened even more. 'I would never do such a low thing!' she protested, trying not to colour guiltily over her earlier vengeful thoughts. 'Never! I have a high regard for achievement and hard work, regardless of what my opinion is of the person behind them.'

'And what is that, if you don't mind my asking?'

'Well, I . . . I . . .'

'Go on, tell me exactly *what* you have against me, except a bit of ancient history that was hardly my fault, regardless of the consequences.' He folded his arms and glared at her. 'Well? Haven't you anything to say? Don't you think I deserve an explanation for this exaggerated hostility?'

Carolyn's mind was going round and round. All she could think of was that fury became him, making him draw his body up tall and straight and proud, making his eyes darken and flash with a wicked appeal, his jaw jutting strongly forward, highlighting the splendid bones in his face.

Only later did she remember that she could have thrown his relationship with Anthea Maxwell in his face. Mrs Maxwell was, after all, a married woman, unlike Miss Powers who was clearly single. But at the time, she merely blushed furiously, giving him a dangerous glimpse of her vulnerability. 'I . . . I don't know,' she said shakily, before pulling herself together and lifting an equally proud chin. 'You seem to bring out the worst in me. You always have done. I just don't like you, Vaughan. I'm sorry, but that's the truth.'

Her blunt remarks surprised him. They rather surprised her too. But after the surprise came self-satisfaction.

At least I'm taking this ridiculous attraction by the scruff of the neck and killing its chances of going anywhere stone dead. Nothing puts a man off more than saying you don't like him.

Not that I really needed to put him off, she thought with a certain irony. He hasn't shown one ounce of interest in me in a sexual sense. Quite understandable, looking as I do today.

'Well, I'm sorry about that too,' he returned brusquely. 'I always rather liked you. Even as a child you had character. You weren't a dither-headed little nincompoop like most of your girlfriends.'

'Oh? You mean because I didn't drool over the gorgeous Vaughan Slater?' she said acidly before she could bite the words back.

His eyes narrowed slightly and Carolyn hoped she hadn't just made a big mistake. Too much hostility was more revealing than none at all. With a supreme effort she dragged up a covering smile. 'See?' she laughed drily. 'You're still bringing out the worst in me. I'm not usually such a bitch.'

Those thoughtful eyes travelled over her so intently that her arms broke out in goose-bumps under her jacket sleeves. 'No,' he said slowly. 'I wouldn't have thought you were. Frankly, I think that if you could put aside this irrational antagonism of yours you'd probably turn into quite the nicest, most sincere person I've ever met.'

Her stomach clenched down hard. First sympathy, and now flattery. Oh, he had all the best weapons where women were concerned, didn't he? Thank God he didn't seem to fancy her or she'd be in real danger.

'You know it will be hard working together, if you're going to be glaring and sniping at me all the time,' he went on quite reasonably. 'Do you think, for the house's sake, you could put your dislike of me on hold for two months? Or is that too long for you to control your—er—feelings?'

Carolyn swallowed. She certainly hoped not. 'I think I could just about manage two months.'

He laughed. 'Good lord, you don't pull any punches do you? But who knows? Once you get to know me better, you might find I'm not quite the heartless cad you've obviously believed I was all these years.'

I doubt that very much, she thought with private irony.

Vaughan's mouth curved back into a rueful smile as he surveyed her unrelenting face. 'Come on. Maddie will be wondering where you are.' And with that he took her elbow again, opened the door, and marched her from the room.

She was jerked to a halt in front of the secretary's desk.

'I'm walking Carolyn here along to Maddie's office, Nora,' Vaughan pronounced. 'I'll be back in five minutes and you'll be able to go home. The big bad ogre is giving you an early mark for putting up with his rudeness.'

'Oh, Mr Slater,' the woman simpered in return. 'You're never really rude.'

His chuckle was dry. 'That's an opinion not shared by several building contractors I know.'

'Some of them deserve a blast,' the secretary defended loyally.

'We had all sorts of trouble with the plumbers at Julian's house,' Vaughan confessed as they made their way along to Suite Four, that insidious male hand still glued to her arm. 'Most of the time they just didn't turn up when they said they would. It's no wonder one can't get a house built in the time scheduled if the tradesmen don't even make an appearance some days.'

'But what excuse do they give?' Carolyn asked, curious, despite her discomfort. She was still shaking inside from their highly strung encounter, and quite rattled by her unexpected response to her once vowed enemy. If only he wouldn't keep on touching her...

Vaughan shrugged his broad shoulders in reply. 'Occasionally the weather. It was either too hot or too cold or too wet, which was crazy since the walls and roof were intact at the time. Mostly they just said they hadn't finished the previous job, but when I contacted the project in question I found out that hadn't been finished because they consistently hadn't turned up there either! It's a vicious circle of apathy and laziness. No wonder this country's building industry is in a mess!'

'You really care about your work, don't you?' she remarked.

His sidewards glance was puzzled. 'You sound surprised. Oh, I see...' His eyes darkened, flashing with anger. 'I'm a man without conscience, without... what was it? Without a shred of decency.' He made a dry, scoffing sound. 'As a man without morals, I'm not supposed to have any integrity, even regarding my work, am I? Might I remind you, Carolyn,' he added caustically, 'that some of the most immoral men in history have been high achievers. Look at Napoleon or Hitler!'

She flinched under his outburst. 'I would *hardly* put you in the same category as Hitler.'

His laughter did not sound amused. He reached out to the doorknob of Suite Four and lanced her with a cynical look. 'Methinks our temporary truce is already fraying at the edges, but I suggest we regroup our defences for Maddie. We don't want her asking any awkward questions, do we?'

'Certainly not.'

'Smile, then, Carolyn. We're about to put your acting ability to the supreme test. Maddie has the most devilish female intuition that sees all, hears all and knows all, if given half a chance. She will not be fooled except by a most convincing performance. How *are* you at acting?'

'Very good, actually,' she returned with a measure of black humour. And gave him an Academy Award-winning smile. If she weren't a good actress, he'd already know she found him the most disturbingly attractive man she'd ever met.

'Excellent. And I presume you want to pretend we've just met for the first time?'

'Definitely.'

'I thought as much,' he muttered, and with a savage twist of his hand flung the door to Suite Four open and waved her inside.

CHAPTER FOUR

'MADDIE, sweetheart,' he called out once they were in the conspicuously empty reception area, 'in which one of your rooms are you hiding?'

A door on the left opened and the most striking-looking woman Carolyn had ever seen appeared. She was very tall—almost as tall as Vaughan—and very slim, with the whitest of white skin. Yet everything else about her was black. Black hair, long and curly, bundled up in a most irregular pony-tail. Black eyes, flashing at the moment with apparent exasperation. Black eyebrows, thick and sardonically arched. Skin-tight black mini dress, black lacy stockings and black high heels. Only her ear-rings were coloured, huge discs in red, pink and orange hanging in interlocking circles from her lobes to her shoulders.

'You're late again!' she accused, giving Vaughan a black look from those striking black eyes.

Carolyn tensed.

'Only by a few minutes,' Vaughan said, and smiled wryly. 'Something not going right for you, sweetheart?' He strode forward and gave the woman a bear-hug. 'You always get testy like this when your colours aren't blending properly.'

'Don't think you can get around me that easily, you bad man,' the interior decorator scorned, but didn't retreat from the hug. 'Save it all for your lady-loves.' And suddenly she winked at Carolyn over his shoulder.

Her heart gave a little jump. Did that mean Vaughan *wasn't* sleeping with this woman?

Dismay was hot on the heels of her avid curiosity. What did it matter who he was sleeping with these days? It should mean nothing to her. *Nothing*!

Self-disgust must have sent a hard look into her face, for those black eyes—which a second before had winked at her—abruptly changed from an expression of amusement to a surprised thoughtfulness. Their owner drew back from Vaughan's embrace to cast a sharp look his way.

'You haven't been bullying this sweet girl, have you?' she asked.

'No. Only Nora.'

'Oh, Vaughan. Truly? The poor woman...'

'Poor, my foot. I pay her damn well to sit there and answer the telephone. Anyway it's all smoothed over now. Carolyn glared at me reproachfully and made me feel guilty, didn't you?' He threw an ironic look her way. 'And it's not Carolyn Thornton, by the way. Her surname is McKensie. She hasn't taken Julian's name.'

'Really? But I thought...'

'So did I. Seems Nora just jumped to that conclusion. Anyway, it's Carolyn McKensie. Carolyn...come over here and meet Maddie.'

Carolyn walked forward and extended her hand. 'How do you do?'

Maddie smiled and took her hand, all the while those penetrating black eyes surveying her closely, seemingly stripping her of her disguising clothes and making Carolyn feel most peculiarly naked. She had never had a woman look at her like that before and a most uncomfortable suspicion sprang into her mind.

'My, you're a very sensual-looking girl, aren't you?' the other woman said. 'I'd love to paint you. In the nude, preferably.'

Carolyn tried not to choke on the spot.

'For God's sake, Maddie!' Vaughan exploded with ill-concealed exasperation. 'What will she start thinking if you say things like that without ex-plaining yourself? Maddie's a well-known portrait artist, Carolyn,' he elaborated wearily, 'special-ising in nudes and semi-nudes. She's been com-missioned to do some quite famous women. *And* men. Believe me when I say she prefers painting the men to the women,' he finished in a dry tone.

'Now you make me sound promiscuous!' Maddie wailed, but without seeming at all put out.

'If the cap fits...'

'Well, if that isn't the pot calling the kettle black,' she countered with a pretend pout.

Carolyn stared from one to the other. This was not the camaraderie of lovers but of old friends. Friends who knew and liked each other, warts and all.

A type of envy tightened Carolyn's chest. She'd never had a friend like that.

But then she glanced at Vaughan and knew that she didn't want him as a friend anyway. She wanted...

A shudder of revulsion and denial shook her.

'I think, Maddie, dear, that we are making Carolyn uncomfortable,' Vaughan said tersely. 'Let's attend to the matter in hand. Julian's house.'

The conversation swiftly focused on business while Vaughan made arrangements for the afternoon. He left shortly after with Carolyn's promise that she would come along and collect him after she'd finished looking at colours and samples.

Maddie sighed expressively once Vaughan was out of earshot. 'Gorgeous hunk of man, that, don't you think?'

A telling heat zoomed into Carolyn's cheeks and the decorator's sharp black eyes rounded slightly.

'I've always found good-looking men best avoided,' Carolyn tossed off, hoping to deflect any unfortunately correct assumptions. 'They're insufferably arrogant. And incorrigibly unfaithful.'

Maddie laughed. 'You could be right, especially on that last bit. But they're also damned interesting, don't you think?'

'Not particularly.'

'Really? How unusual. Well, at least you won't get hurt that way. Of course, you might also be bored to death, but who am I to judge?' She laughed delightfully. 'I'm thirty years old and haven't managed to hold on to a single, solitary good-looking man in my whole adult life. Still...I'm not complaining. They were all fun while they lasted and, to be frank, I'm not interested in marriage. Most married women look frightfully bored, don't you think?'

Without waiting for an answer, she whirled and started walking towards a different door from the one she'd first come out of. 'Follow me.' She waved over her shoulder. 'I'll show you the colour scheme I've chosen. Then the samples for the carpet and furniture. When you see the house later this afternoon you'll be able to picture what goes where.'

Carolyn was relieved to get off the subject of Maddie's private life. Not to mention Vaughan's.

She traipsed after the tall, thin figure, thinking that, despite not approving of Maddie's casual attitude to men and sex, she was still drawn to the other woman's personality. Perhaps because Maddie was everything *she* wasn't. Gay and carefree and uninhibited. Next to her, Carolyn felt very much the prim and proper, prickly virgin she probably looked.

And yet... Maddie had seen through her disguise, had called her sensual-looking, had wanted to paint her. Against all common sense, Carolyn was both flattered and tempted to take her up on the invitation. Perhaps if she could cast off her clothes as nonchalantly as she was sure Maddie could, she might stop being so uptight, especially when it came to the opposite sex.

Don't be ridiculous, her real self returned briskly. Posing for a nude painting is not you. Not you at all. What on earth's got into you today? First, going all watery-kneed over a man you despise, just because he has a handsome face, a bewitching smile and a body any woman would itch to get her hands on. And now, to cap it all off, wanting to act like some Bohemian.

She threw a rueful look at Maddie leaning over the large desk in her skin-tight dress, those outrageous ear-rings swinging about her shoulders. The day you can feel comfortable in *that* rig-out will be the day you pose nude. Which is *never*!

'Well, what do you think?'

Carolyn jolted out of her mental arguings to re-alise that Maddie had been talking all the while, and laying out a whole spectrum of colour squares on the desk top. They ranged from crisp light blues to more vibrant violets to a deep ocean green, alongside a surprisingly attractive apricot-fawn. They were cool, classical colours which would never jar or offend, but had enough character not to look insipid. She hated houses that were painted all white, or all cream, like hospital rooms. Her mother did too.

'This is for the living areas,' Maddie said, pointing to the fawn. 'Ceilings to be wood-panelled. The other colours are for various bedrooms and bathrooms. Ceilings to be ivory. No wallpaper. It changes fashion too quickly.'

'I *love* these colours,' Carolyn praised enthusiastically.

'You surprise me,' was the almost teasing reply. 'I thought, looking at your clothes, that you might favour something a little less...bright. Or am I right in guessing this isn't your usual garb?'

Carolyn had to laugh. Maddie was as intuitive as Vaughan had said. 'You could be half right there.'

'Only *half*?'

'This is my office image. I—er—don't like to at-tract attention where I work.'

'Aah... A man...'

Carolyn nodded.

'And you came here from work today?'

'Oh, no, I——' Too late, she bit her tongue.

'Ah... I see... You came here dressed like that because you didn't want to attract Vaughan.'

She was *far* too intuitive, Carolyn conceded unhappily. 'Julian did warn me about him,' she admitted.

'And rightly so,' Maddie agreed blithely. 'Vaughan's not for the likes of you, dear girl. Best you keep wearing maidenly suits like that every time you're around him.'

Carolyn was intrigued, despite herself. 'Why do you say he isn't for the likes of me?'

'Because you're a nice girl and he's a bastard. Sleeps with every attractive woman who makes a line for him, has them running round like chooks with their heads cut off, mothering him, pandering to his every whim. And then what happens? He gets involved in a new project and forgets them. Stands them up without meaning to or doesn't turn up till he's hours late. He drives them insane with jealousy and insecurity till they dump him in despair. But does he care? Not a scrap. Just shrugs and goes on working till the next silly female throws herself at his head and it all starts over again.'

'But hasn't he ever fallen in love?' she questioned, appalled yet fascinated.

'Never.'

'And he's no desire for marriage and children?'

'Not that I know of. Of course he's a typical male when it comes to talking about himself. He's about as easy to open up as a rock oyster. My God, I shared a flat with him in Sydney for three years and in all that time I never even found out when his birthday was. Still don't know.'

'You . . . you were lovers?' Carolyn asked, her chest tightening.

'Actually...no.' She sounded as surprised as Carolyn felt. 'Don't ask me why. After all, he's a sexy beast and I'm hardly a dog, am I?' she quipped without batting an eyelash. 'I think it was because I was involved with another man when we first met. And Vaughan was going through one of his anti-social moods. By the time he snapped out of it and I'd broken up with my current love, we'd become friends. Hard to feel passion for an old friend, especially one you've seen looking their worst. Anyway, he wasn't into women so much back then. Just work. He had three jobs. Slogged away for a large architectural firm during the day, and moon-lighted as a bar-tender at night, and a lifeguard at the weekend. Brother, talk about a workaholic! Still is.'

'And do you still share accommodation?'

'God, no! Three years was enough of that macho slob. I have my own sweet little house now, right on the beach at Thirroul. *Very* tastefully furnished and decorated, I might add.'

'Thirroul? Where's that?'

'North of Bulli. Lovely spot. A bit windy but where isn't it along the south coast?'

'And Vaughan?' Carolyn probed. 'Where does he live?'

'*Live*?' Maddie squawked. 'Vaughan doesn't *live* anywhere. He dosses down in a ramshackle old house he bought on the cliffs overlooking the sea at Austinmere. And before you ask, that's the next beach north from Thirroul. Well, hardly a beach. More a cove, in my opinion. Actually, Vaughan's place is on a terrific block of land—view-wise—but the house always looks as if a bomb has hit it.

Except, of course, when one of his women goes into their mothering act and cleans up for him. He keeps saying he's going to renovate the place but never gets round to it. There's always a new project to work on for a paying customer, which he finds infinitely preferable to a job one would have to pay for oneself.'

'I can imagine,' Carolyn muttered bitterly. 'Leopards don't change their spots, do they?'

Maddie's startled reaction communicated itself to Carolyn and she gave a soft groan of dismay. Me and my big mouth! she thought.

'You know Vaughan, don't you?' came the inevitable question. 'From the past... And he's done something to hurt you.'

'No, no,' she denied in a fluster. 'Please... I... I don't really know him. I... I know someone who knew him and yes, he did hurt her. But unintentionally, I think. Look, I don't want to talk about it, Maddie. I want to forget it. Vaughan does too. *Please* don't mention it to him that I slipped up.'

'If that's what you want...'

'Yes, it is.'

Maddie sighed and gathered up the colour cards. 'Right. In that case we'd better move on to the fabrics I've chosen for the curtains and furnishing. And the carpet samples.'

Carolyn liked everything she was shown. Maddie had the most superbly elegant taste, never using the stripes and fussy florals Carolyn knew her mother disliked. The carpet to be laid in the formal living areas and bedrooms was to be a darker shade of the apricot-fawn to be used on the living-room walls, and blended beautifully with the more vi-

brant colours Maddie had chosen for the bedrooms. The more heavily used family areas were to
be tiled with a black African slate that was both
fantastic to look at and extremely serviceable. There
wasn't a thing Isabel would object to.

Finally, she was shown pictures and brochures of
the furniture which was about to be ordered. All
very classical and rich looking with simple clean
lines and dark wood, and lots of leather.

'You can change anything you think your mother
won't like,' Maddie assured her. 'Please don't think
you'll hurt my feelings if you speak up.'

'But I wouldn't change a thing. Not a thing!'

Maddie laughed. 'I wish all my clients were as
agreeable as you. They hire me, but they quickly
forget that this is my profession. It's what I've been
trained to do. I *should* be able to choose better than
the average person. But usually, they have some pet
likes they want included that totally ruins the effect
I want, and I have to go through all sorts of reverse
psychology to get my way. You can't just give them
a look of horror and say, Oh, God no! It's always,
Yes, that's very nice but unfortunately... Or, Oh,
do you think so? Poor Mrs Whatsername chose
something similar and she was most disappointed
by the finish. Sent it back, et cetera et cetera.'

A knock on the office door startled them both.
Maddie walked over to open it and a large woman
in a ghastly floral dress was standing there, looking
decidedly impatient.

'I waited for ten minutes outside, Miss Powers,
but it's now ten past noon and I...'

'Oh, goodness, is it? I am so sorry, Mrs
Makepiece,' she said, and threw the lady a winning

smile. 'I do so get carried away when I work. Please come in. Carolyn and I are finished for now.' She showed the woman over to a chair and hurried back behind the desk. 'I'll see you at the house at two,' she whispered to Carolyn. 'You go along and have lunch with Vaughan, and don't let him get under your skin. He's quite harmless really, as long as you keep him at arm's length.'

'Will do,' she returned with a conspiratorial smile. Yes, she liked this woman. Very much indeed. There was an unpretentiousness, a natural freshness about her that was almost catching. Perhaps if she stayed around her long enough, she might pluck up the courage for that painting.

Carolyn hurried back along the corridor, aware she'd taken longer than Vaughan had expected her to and hoping he hadn't minded waiting. He wasn't the calmest of customers when it came to his work and she could see him in her mind, pacing up and down, glaring at his watch, muttering impatiently.

At least her time spent talking with Maddie had put her response to Vaughan into better perspective. He was one of those men who bowled women over, quite naturally, and without much effort on his part. His looks plus his air of apparent indifference to the opposite sex added up to an irresistible challenge. Women apparently ran after him, not the other way around. And when in the mood, he was only too happy to oblige them.

Carolyn had never met a man before with such a strongly magnetic sexual aura and she hadn't been prepared for it, that was all. Now that she'd had time and space to gather her senses, she felt confident she could handle the situation much better.

Vaughan wasn't pacing up and down. Far from it. He was settled behind that mess of a desk of his, working away so obsessively that he didn't even hear Carolyn come in. For a long moment, she just watched him, bent over with his pencil and ruler in his hands, the tip of his tongue resting at the corner of his mouth as he painstakingly went about ruling very precise lines. He looked like a boy she'd seen once, playing marbles in the gutter, a picture of concentration as he went about winning all the other boys' marbles.

Maddie was wrong, Carolyn decided as she watched him. Vaughan *had* fallen in love. With his work. Architecture was his love, his real mistress. Women were nothing but a leisure pleasure, a momentary relaxation, a rest and recreation activity till he got back to what mattered most in his life. Planning and designing.

'Vaughan.'

He almost jumped out of his skin. 'Good God, don't *do* that! You almost gave me a heart attack.'

'Sorry.'

'What time is it?'

'A quarter after twelve.'

'Already? I thought I'd only been here five minutes.' He scratched his head with the end of his pencil, but not a hair was displaced. With his short spiked style, he could have put a wheat harvester through it and it wouldn't have made much difference.

'Can you wait five more minutes?' he asked, frowning back down at his work.

'Sure.' She settled back into the black plastic chair, trying vainly to ignore the fact that, against all her best intentions, she was gaining some weird pleasure from just being in the same room as this man. Her heart was definitely beating faster and she just couldn't take her eyes off him, couldn't stop gazing at his handsome face, his sensual mouth, his elegant hands.

I'm crazy, she decided. I know what he is, *who* he is. And yet...

Guilt began to consume her in waves as the minutes ticked by. How can I be feeling like this about the man who almost destroyed my mother—however unwittingly? Why can't I control my feelings, my bodily reactions? What kind of a daughter *am* I?

Twenty minutes later Vaughan looked up and caught her still staring at him, no doubt looking as troubled as she felt. Luckily, once he glanced at his watch, he interpreted it as something very different from what it was.

'Oh, good grief,' he groaned, 'why didn't you say something? Hell, I'm hopeless when I work.' He jumped to his feet and snatched up a couple of keys from under some papers. 'Let's go. I'll pick up some takeaway and eat it at the house, otherwise Maddie will almost get there before we do.'

Vaughan locked up then bustled Carolyn down the stairs and out into the sunlight. The day had warmed up considerably since she'd gone inside and the heat hit her quite forcibly. February in Australia and long woollen sleeves did not mix.

She groaned and Vaughan's eyes swung her way, sweeping up and down her body. 'You'd be much more comfortable without that jacket on.'

'Perhaps,' she returned shortly. 'But I . . . I burn easily. Does your car have air-conditioning?'

'Sort of,' he grinned wryly.

God, did he have to look like that when he smiled? Why couldn't he have crooked yellow teeth or something? 'What do you mean . . . sort of?'

'You'll find out soon enough.'

He drove a rather ancient maroon MG, with the top down, which would have made a fiasco of any woman's hair that wasn't plaited and pinned down with the security of Fort Knox. He was a good driver, but impatient, nipping from lane to lane, passing any vehicle that didn't do the speed limit, and generally giving Carolyn quite a few adrenalin surges.

Not at all what she needed. Her heart was already pumping away like the Snowy Mountain Hydro-Electric Scheme at full throttle. Guilt, she finally accepted, was no weapon against a fatal sexual attraction.

'Won't be a moment,' he said as he zipped into a takeaway chicken place. 'I'll get you a thick shake. Or would you prefer a Coke?'

'A thick shake would be fine.'

'Strawberry or chocolate?'

'Either.'

'Are you sure you don't want something to eat?'

'Well . . . maybe a small chicken burger.' She *was* beginning to feel a bit hungry, despite everything.

'Dieting, are we?' he teased, but gave her well-disguised figure a curious look before alighting, typically without opening the car door.

In five minutes he was back with a large plastic bag and a cardboard tray with four drinks balancing in it. 'Here...' He dumped the plastic bag in the back and handed her the drinks. 'Put these on your knee and don't let them spill.'

Jawohl, mein Kommandant, she said in her mind. Out loud she muttered thanks and observed that there were two chocolate and two strawberry milk-shakes in her lap. One thing was for sure. He wasn't mean.

'How far from here to Julian's house?' she enquired as he hurdled over the driver's door back into the car with infuriating grace. Not for *him* the clumsy trip that would send him splattering all over the drinks in her lap.

'Not far at all. That's it up there,' he pointed, gesturing high up into the hills behind them. 'The concrete and glass place way up on its own.'

Carolyn's eyes lifted to fasten on Julian's wedding gift to her mother. It was a house like no other she'd ever seen, a triple storeyed semi-circular structure with huge windows sparkling in the sunlight. But what made it even more spectacular was its location. Virtually on the side of a cliff, it hugged the rockface, like a mountain-climber.

'How does it stay up there?' she asked, her voice awed.

'By the miracle of steel struts and poles. Haven't you heard of pole houses? Well, this one's just taken that principle a little further than usual.'

'A lot further, I would say. Gosh, it must have a magnificent view from those front balconies.'

'It does.'

'But where did you put the pool? Julian said it had a pool. I can't see where it would fit.'

'It's built into the roof.'

'*Really*?'

He twisted to face her, smiling broadly at her almost childish astonishment. '*Really*. Shall we go and eat our takeaway, pool-side?'

'You mean it has water in it already?'

'Not yet,' he laughed. 'But it *does* have sides.'

She laughed as well, her head tipping back with automatic delight. But when she turned sparkling blue eyes towards Vaughan she saw his own eyes widen with surprise, saw them drop to fasten on her laughing mouth. The jolting remembrance of just who she was laughing with, whose company she was enjoying more than any other man in all her life sobered her immediately, all laughter wiped from her face in an instant.

Vaughan's sigh was full of irritation. 'For pity's sake, can't you relax long enough around me to have a simple laugh? I'm not Bluebeard, you know. Truly, Carolyn, I don't understand you at all!'

'Don't you?' she said bitterly.

'No. What the hell do you think really happened between me and your mother all those years ago? God, anybody would think I raped her or something!'

Bringing up her mother in that tone revitalised all her earlier vengeful anger. She twisted in the seat to face him, cheeks hot, blue eyes derisive. 'Oh, I appreciate you wouldn't have to do that, Vaughan Slater. Not *you*! Women throw themselves at you, don't they? All you do is go around flashing that devastating smile of yours these days and they drop at your feet like flies. You don't even have to take your shirt off!

'Well, let me tell you this,' she went on a dark, trembling voice, 'you can flash your pearly whites my way till the cows come home and you won't turn *my* head. So do what Maddie suggested and save your selective brand of charm for your lady-loves. After all, you'd be wasting your time with me. I don't have any money or anything else you could possibly want! Keep to the Anthea Maxwells of this world. They're well suited to men like you!'

If Carolyn hadn't been blindly furious herself she might have been frightened by the look that came into his eyes. Or by the cold fury in his voice. 'And *I* suggest you explain that last remark or else get out of this car right now.'

Her mouth dropped open, only then realising just how rude she had been. But she refused to back down, snapping her mouth shut and glaring at him quite boldly. 'Very well. You might as well know exactly what I think of you and why. I'm already fed up trying to be civil to you when what I would really like to do is slap your arrogant face for what you did to my mother.'

Her top lip curled with contempt. 'Oh, yes, I know you didn't force yourself upon her or anything so crass. But the truth is, Vaughan, you're an incorrigible womaniser, encouraging women to fall in love with you without caring a hoot if they eventually get hurt. You're blind to other people's feelings, which is why I said you were suited to women like Anthea Maxwell. She's equally selfish. And equally immoral. *She* won't have a nervous breakdown when you walk away. Far from it. She'd merely move on to the next stud she can find. Or *buy*.'

His whole face tightened at this last barb, but he said nothing in his own defence, his gaze livid. Carolyn lifted her chin defiantly and swept on. 'Having said all that, I'm quite prepared to get out of this car, if that's what you still want. But my beef is with *you*, not Maddie, and she'll be expecting us both at the house shortly. I don't think it's fair to involve her in our personal problems.'

'Neither do I,' he ground at her. 'Neither do I...'

For a long, long minute he kept glaring at her, before saying abruptly, 'Are you religious?'

The unexpected change of subject threw her. 'No! Well, yes...I *am* a Christian, but I...I don't go to church on any regular basis. Why?'

'I was just wondering...'

'Wondering *what*?' she demanded to know.

'Why you find sexual relationships between consenting adults immoral? Or why you're so disapproving of Anthea Maxwell?'

Her laughter was full of incredulity. 'Haven't you forgotten one small factor?'

'Have I?'

'Yes... *Mr* Maxwell.'

Vaughan looked puzzled. 'Arthur?'

'If that's what he's called. Don't you think he might object to your sleeping with his wife?'

She was appalled by the wry smile that crossed Vaughan's face. 'Nope.'

'Oh, I see,' she scorned. 'He's as immoral as you are, is that it?'

He sucked in a sharp breath, then exhaled slowly. 'Not exactly, Carolyn. Though he was well known for his...dalliances. But the main reason Arthur Maxwell wouldn't object is because he's dead. Has been for two years.'

CHAPTER FIVE

'OH...'

Carolyn dropped her eyes to stare blankly down at the drinks in her lap, embarrassed colour sweeping up her neck and into her face.

'Only oh?' Vaughan said coldly. 'Don't you think you owe me an apology?'

She said nothing, refusing to concede any such thing. Just because he hadn't committed adultery with Mrs Maxwell, it didn't mean he hadn't with other female clients. Maddie had implied that he slept with every woman who threw herself at him, and she was sure some of them would have been married.

'I wonder what other dark sins you've attributed to me in that warped mind of yours?' he snarled. 'Besides being a callous seducer and adulterer, that is.'

Carolyn lifted her eyes and swung them his way. 'As you said to Maddie, Vaughan. If the cap fits...'

'And what caps fit you, Carolyn? The cap of intolerance? Prejudice? Narrow-mindedness?'

'If it's narrow-minded not to like men who use women for their own selfish ends without the tiniest scrap of real caring, then I *am* narrow-minded. I won't deny it.'

'I've never used any woman who didn't want to be used, I assure you,' he said darkly. 'Women are not always whiter than white, dear girl. Pity you haven't realised that.'

Carolyn bristled. 'Are you referring to my mother?'

His sigh carried a weary resignation. 'No, I am not. For God's sake, can we get off the subject of your mother? I'm sorry for what happened to her. Terribly sorry. But that episode is dead and buried and I refuse to feel any false guilt. I also refuse to let you throw that up in my face all the time. I won't have it, do you hear me?'

'Me, and the rest of Wollongong!'

He flushed darkly when he noticed several people at a nearby car staring over at them. Muttering, he fired the engine and screeched out of the car park, burning rubber. Carolyn was glad of the lids on the drinks or they'd have spilt everywhere.

'I would like to get home tonight in one piece,' she bit out when they skidded round the next corner.

'Why?' he snapped. 'It's not as though you've got a date.'

Her sideways glance was startled. Then annoyed. 'And why *wouldn't* I have a date?'

His returning look was full of contempt. 'Because you're far too uptight and self-righteous. Far too anti-men. Good lord, just look at you, done up like a maiden aunt, projecting a prickly aloofness most of the time that would scare a man off from a hundred yards. You became human briefly back there in the car park. In fact, you actually looked like a vibrant, attractive young woman for a few seconds before you buttoned up your sexuality again. If you've got a date tonight, honey, then I'm a monkey's uncle.'

'Is that so? Well, I'll have you know that——'

'Oh, save it, sweetheart, I'm not interested. Let's just get up to the house and get this over and done with as soon as possible. And I suggest you deal through Maddie in future. By the end of today I'll have had about as much of you as I can take.'

Carolyn was running late for work the following Monday morning, due to having slept in. Her body clock had been well and truly put out by not being able to sleep at all on the Saturday night after her return from Wollongong. Sunday had been no more restful, all attempts to have a much needed nap failing. By the time her head hit the pillow that night she'd been too tired to do anything but sleep. And sleep. And sleep.

An irritable sigh punched from her lips as the traffic lights ahead changed to red. Damn it, she thought. If she'd caught one red light, she'd caught them all.

The trip from her unit in Ashfield out along the Hume Highway to Warwick Farm and the private hospital where she worked could take anything from twenty minutes to an hour, depending on the traffic. This morning's was horrendous, compounding her tardiness, as was her being extra careful with Julian's car. She would have driven her old bomb if she'd been able to get it to start, but a flat battery had been her undoing.

She stopped at the lights and glanced in the rear-view mirror, groaning when she saw her hair. It was a mess! But she just hadn't had time to plait it

She'd barely had time to shower and throw on some clothes before racing out of the door at eight-thirty. Normally she was gone by eight at the latest.

I'll bolt into the ladies' room as soon as I get to work and do it properly, she resolved.

Hunger pangs in her stomach also told Carolyn that she hadn't eaten any breakfast. Actually, she hadn't eaten much for two days.

'Damn Vaughan Slater,' she muttered aloud. 'Damn, damn, damn!'

Her mind flashed back to the strained hour she'd spent with him and Maddie at Julian's house, a house which, when it was finished, would indeed be magnificent. But it wasn't the house that had filled her thoughts for long after she'd left Wollongong. It was Vaughan, the man who'd once haunted her mother; who was now haunting her.

He hadn't bothered to hide his annoyance with her, even in Maddie's presence, using a hard, almost mocking tone to point out the various features of the house.

Maddie noticed, of course, giving both of them wide-eyed curious glances all the time. Finally, Vaughan announced that he had to leave, that he had things to do before going to Anthea's party that night, at which Maddie spun round from where she was standing across the large living-room, an astonished look on her face.

'You're going to a *party*?'

Vaughan's mouth curved back into an ironic smile. 'Not any party, Maddie. *Anthea's*. Don't worry, she'll make the sacrifice worthwhile,' he drawled and turned to give Carolyn beside him a taunting look. 'Have you seen enough for today?'

With the greatest difficulty she held his gaze, a contemptuous smirk lifting the corner of her mouth. 'More than enough, I would say.'

Her stomach fluttered at the wickedly dangerous anger that flashed into his eyes. She should have known better than to throw out a challenge to a man without conscience. His gaze raked brutally down over her body, then up again. 'I can't say the same in return,' he murmured, so low that Maddie would not have heard. 'But one day, Carolyn. One day...'

She sucked in an alarmed breath. Yet alongside the fear lay another, more insidious response.

Desire...

Hers, not his, sparked by the smouldering sensuality of his hard scrutiny, and the sexual threat behind his words. Yet Vaughan did not really want her, she realised wretchedly. All he wanted was to make her eat her words, to tear down her moral resistance by getting her to go to bed with him.

It was this promise of a vengeful seduction that had kept her awake all Saturday night and had churned away in her stomach all Sunday, destroying her appetite and her peace of mind.

Because he could so easily do it, she'd finally accepted. So damned easily.

The lights turned green and she edged the BMW forward, her hands trembling on the wheel. If she kept this up she wouldn't get any sleep tonight either!

It was twenty past nine by the time she pulled the BMW into her slot in the hospital staff car park and turned off the engine. Still agitated over her mind-numbing realisation, Carolyn was all fingers and thumbs as she alighted, first her keys then her carry-all clattering to the concrete. Cursing, she bent to pick them up and her long hair fell forward round her face, some across her eyes, some into her mouth.

Her curse was no longer silent. Neither was it very ladylike.

A man's laughter had her head jerking round to find a pair of elegantly trousered legs standing beside her. Before she could glance up further, their owner crouched down to help her pick up her things.

'Th... thank you,' she stammered.

They rose simultaneously and Carolyn saw that the gallantry belonged to none other than Maurice Jenkins.

'Good lord,' he exclaimed once he recognised her. 'It's Carolyn McKensie from Admittance!' Surprised blue eyes began caressing the long fair hair cascading over her shoulders. 'Who would have believed so much gorgeous sexy hair was hiding behind the way you usually wear it?'

Carolyn felt her temper begin to fray immediately. It surprised her. She was not normally so touchy. Or easy to rile. 'Amazing, isn't it?' she returned with gritted teeth.

'You should wear it loose more often.'

'Hardly practical, I'm afraid. Well, I must be going...'

'I thought you drove an old green Datsun,' he cut in, frowning at the BMW.

'Yes, I do.'

'Using the boyfriend's car today?' he smirked.

'That's right,' Carolyn lied. Anything to get this obnoxious man off the scent. God, he was all hot eyes, undressing her, practically raping her in advance. How all those nurses fell for him she had no idea. At least when Vaughan had looked at her he hadn't *leered*.

The doctor's surprise at her admission annoyed her so much that she launched into a further outrageous twisting of semi-truths. 'My car wouldn't start this morning so he gave me his. That's why I'm late.' She indulged in a meaningful feminine giggle. 'Well, that's not entirely true. We—er—*I*...did sleep in, just a little. My weekend was positively exhausting.'

Carolyn gained malicious pleasure from the astonishment that crossed the doctor's weakly handsome face. The thought came to her that, compared to Vaughan's strong features, this man's looks were positively insipid!

The realisation that twice within the last few seconds she had thought favourably of Vaughan rankled her considerably. For pity's sake, you vowed to put that man out of your mind, she lectured herself fiercely.

Easier said than done...

'Please excuse me, Doctor, but I must get into work. I'm late enough as it is.'

As she went to walk past him, he put a staying hand on her arm. She stiffened and looked up at him, ice in her eyes.

He tried one of his supposedly winning smiles on her. It failed abysmally.

'I just wanted to say,' came the silkily delivered line, 'that I've always liked you, Carolyn, and if there's anything you ever need—a shoulder to cry on, perhaps?—then I'll always be there for you. Just give me a call. You must know my number. It's in the files. Promise me you'll do that?' he finished smarmily, and let his hand slide down her arm and back to his side.

God, but he was *revolting*! Carolyn just stopped herself in time from shuddering.

Pasting a false smile on her face, she moved away without saying a word. She didn't trust herself to.

The whole office looked up in open-mouthed unison when she hurried in, not only late but with her hair still down and flying every which way. All eyes focused on the wayward blonde locks.

'Not a word!' she warned them. 'Not a single solitary word! It's going back up in five seconds' time and it will never ever come down again!'

And with that she spun round on her heels and marched from the room.

That week was excruciatingly long. And awfully lonely. Especially once the weekend came round and Carolyn didn't even have work to fill the day. Sleeping was still a problem and she rose early on the Saturday morning, giving herself added hours to find something to do.

After doing her weekly shopping—which was minimal for one person—Carolyn spent more time than usual cleaning the flat, just for something to do. But when she started rearranging perfectly tidy drawers out of sheer boredom she sat down on her bed with a disgruntled sigh.

'Good God, what am I doing this for?'

She shook her head, only then appreciating how much she'd always relied on her mother for

company, how she'd neglected to form the sort of
close friendships that would have stood her in good
stead at times like these.

Oh, yes, she played competitive tennis in the
winter and went out with the ladies A-grade team
for a drink after the game each week. But she didn't
keep in social contact with these girls over the
summer. She *did* go out with the people from work
every once in a while, especially leading up to
Christmas. And of course there had been occasional dates with men in the past.

But lately, her only regular outings at weekends
had been with her mother, either going shopping
or to the beach or the movies. She also ac-
companied Julian and her mother down to the local
club most Saturday nights for dinner, or to enjoy
whatever entertainment was on that week. That club
had been the mainstay of Carolyn and Isabel's
limited social life for years.

It was there that Isabel had met Julian at a dinner
dance, and also where Carolyn herself had met the
few men she'd dated in the past. Though she hadn't
gone out with a man now for over six months. Not
because she hadn't been approached lately, but because she'd come to believe that most men who
picked up women in clubs weren't interested in a
real relationship. They were looking for a one-night
stand.

No matter how lonely Carolyn felt, she wasn't
going to be reduced to *that* way of life!

The unexpected jangling of the phone made her
jump off the bed. Now who could that be? she
wondered, and hurried from the bedroom. But she
couldn't think of anyone who would ring her. As

she approached the telephone table, the sudden thought that something might have gone wrong with Julian and Isabel made her heart flip over.

'Yes?' she answered, unable to keep the worry from her voice.

'It's Vaughan, Carolyn.'

Her shocked intake of breath was quite audible.

'Please don't hang up,' he raced on tautly. 'I must speak with you.'

'W...why?' she stammered, her whole insides contracting. 'Has something gone wrong with the house?'

He gave a short, dry laugh. 'Not at all. If anything, things have never been better in that regard. The plasterers came on time and so did the painters.'

'Well, what did you want to speak to me about?' she demanded, shock and tension making her sharp.

His sigh sounded regretful. 'I've been thinking about what happened last week between you and me, Carolyn...'

'*Nothing* happened between you and me. And nothing's going to!' Cool it, a little voice warned her. You're over the top here.

'If you hang up on me,' he said in a low, measured tone, 'you'll find me on your doorstep.'

Carolyn's eyes almost popped out of her head. Vaughan? Here? In *person*? A phone call, however fraught with tension, was infinitely preferable to *that*!

But she had to pull herself together.

'I have no intention of hanging up, Vaughan. Not unless you force me to.'

'Why in God's name would I do that?' he said impatiently. 'Look, all I wanted was to say how sorry I am things got out of hand last Saturday. It's bothered me all week. I've been trying to see things from your point of view and I can understand part of your attitude towards me. You obviously went through a traumatic experience as a child with Isabel breaking down the way she did, and it's only logical that I would be the object of a lot of anger in your mind. But I ask you in all fairness not to judge me so rashly and harshly when it comes to the way I live my life now. I might not live up to your rather old-fashioned moral standards, but neither am I the blackguard you painted me. I dare say the truth lies somewhere in between,' he finished, and sighed again.

A silence, heavy and expectant, dropped on to the line.

'Carolyn?' he said at last. 'Are you still there?'

'Yes.'

'Did you listen to what I said? *Really* listen?'

'Yes.'

'Well?'

'Well what?'

He made an impatient sound. 'Well, do you agree you might have been a bit hasty in your opinion of me?' he bit out.

'No.'

'Oh, for God's sake!'

'But I do agree things got out of hand. And I do feel guilty that I was so rude. I promise not to be in the future.'

'Do you think that's what I want from you? Icy politeness?'

A surge of excitement shot through her till she pulled herself up short.

This is Vaughan Slater here. My mother's ex-lover, Anthea Maxwell's *present* lover! Also the man who looked at you with such wicked resolve last Saturday and vowed, 'One day, Carolyn... One day...'

'I don't want you to want *anything* from me, Vaughan,' she said with an unfortunately shaking voice.

'You always take everything I say the wrong way!' he protested.

'Do I? I would have to have been deaf, dumb and blind not to know what you threatened me with the other day.'

'That was anger talking,' he ground out. 'I'm not really planning to seduce you!'

'You wouldn't have a hope in Hades, anyway.'

'So I've gathered, believe me.'

His dry mocking tone riled her considerably. 'I'll have you know, Vaughan Slater, that I don't always look and act the way I did on Saturday.'

'If you say so. Maddie certainly seemed to think you had another side to you.'

'But you don't agree with her!' she said tartly.

'I just think it's a travesty that a girl as basically lovely as yourself has become so bitter and twisted when it comes to men and sex.'

'I am *not* bitter and twisted about men and sex!'

'Aren't you?' he murmured, almost sadly. 'Look, we're getting off the point of this call again. My sole intention was to apologise and to smooth the way for us to work together without biting each other's heads off. I also wanted to tell you that by next weekend you'll be able to see the completed interior of the house. Just give me a time suited to you, and Maddie and I'll meet you there at the house.'

Carolyn's head whirled. 'Oh, but I ... I'm not sure if I ...'

'Maybe you would like to check your social diary?'

Perhaps he wasn't being sarcastic, but Carolyn didn't hear it that way. Every word seemed to be full of cynical irony, taunting her, baiting her.

'That won't be necessary,' she answered brusquely. 'Make it at two again on the Saturday afternoon.'

'Fine. And Carolyn,' he added just before hanging up, 'if it's hot, bring your swimming cossie. I'm having the pool filled this week.'

CHAPTER SIX

IT WAS hot. *Very* hot. So hot that to wear something like the grey woollen suit would have been ridiculous.

The day actually called for shorts, a breezy top and sandals. And, in the end, that was what Carolyn wore, reasoning that if she wasn't as normal and natural as possible Vaughan would begin thinking she had something more to hide than her figure.

Still, as she drove into Wollongong her stomach began fluttering with nerves. Would Vaughan insist on that swim after they'd inspected the house? And if he did, would she go along with the idea? After all, that would mean wearing the costume lying in the beach bag on the passenger seat, a costume which, though a reasonably modest black one-piece, wouldn't hide much of her body.

Carolyn had never been able to work out just why men found her body so desirable. She wasn't tall with long sexy legs. She didn't have big breasts. Neither was her bottom lushly rounded. If anything, her figure was rather boyish in its slightness.

But she did have an exceptionally tiny waist, which she supposed lent an illusion of extra curves to the rest of her. And her skin always acquired that softly golden hue in summer that seemed to impel men to touch it.

Carolyn had learnt over the years to be careful in what she wore, for she did so hate being subjected to wolf whistles and leering stares and unwanted pawing. Which was why her wardrobe was mostly full of clothes designed to detract from, rather than enhance her figure. The few exceptions were her mother's choices, not her own.

The shorts set she was wearing today was a borderline case. It had been a Christmas present from Julian, chosen no doubt by Isabel. Simple white cotton Bermuda shorts with cuffs made in the same geometric pink and white material as the matching top.

It was not a sexy outfit by any stretch of the imagination, but the shorts did have a wide belt which emphasised her small waist, and the singlet-style top exposed all her arms and a great deal of her slender shoulders. With her hair dangling down her back in a single loose plait and pink lip gloss on, Carolyn knew she was presenting a very feminine picture, a far cry from the old-maidish image she'd dished up to Vaughan a fortnight before.

Nevertheless, what am I worrying about? she argued dismissively. He's not attracted to me in the slightest. He thinks I'm twisted, *sexless*! More than likely he'll make some sarcastic comment about my changed appearance then set about mocking me for the rest of the time we have to spend together.

Which brought her back to his asking her to bring her swimming costume. Why had he? she worried for the umpteenth time. Did he have some devious ulterior motive? Or was it just a 'let-bygones-be-bygones' gesture?

The road that led up to Julian's house was very steep. It wound up into the hills behind Wollongong till it was actually above the house, since a driveway directly up the cliff-face below would have been impossible. The third floor of the house—or rooftop—was just below the level of the road and housed four carports behind which stood the courtyard which held the pool and surrounds. A wide staircase dropped from the roof down to the next level which consisted of general living areas. Another staircase took one down to the sleeping quarters of four bedrooms, all with matching en-suites. Both lower levels sported huge semi-circular balconies that faced out to the sea in the distance.

Vaughan's MG was already parked in one of the carports when Carolyn drew up to the house, just the sight of it twisting her insides into instant knots. Her reaction annoyed her. How could she appear normal and natural if she was wound up so tight she'd probably snap at the most innocuous comment he made?

Her eyes swept round for a sight of Maddie's black car, but it was conspicuously absent. Carolyn began hoping Vaughan might have brought Maddie with him.

Apparently he hadn't, for he strode out alone as soon as she turned off the engine.

Her heart turned over when she saw him, for he was only half-dressed, his gorgeously tanned body displayed heart-stoppingly in white shorts and not another single damned thing. No top. No shoes. Nothing. He looked as if he'd just emerged from a cooling swim, deep brown hair slicked back at the sides and spiky on top, bronzed skin still glistening.

A huge lump claimed her throat as she watched him stride purposefully towards her side of the car, his hand reaching out to open the door for her. She was so rattled by the way her heart started thudding in her chest that she wasn't at all prepared for the way he looked at *her* once she forced her heavy legs out from behind the wheel.

An odd stillness claimed him. He stared, without seeming to breathe, only his eyes moving. It was the most devastatingly intense scrutiny she'd ever been subjected to.

Oh, God, Carolyn thought.

Just when she began to panic, his face relaxed into a sardonic smile. 'I see you're intent on making me eat my words,' he drawled, and shut the car door behind her. 'Not only do I now know you've got a figure as dainty and delicate as a crystal hourglass, but you've also taken that awful bun thing down.' His hands reached out to hold her by the shoulders and turn her round to inspect the single plait dangling down her back. 'Still plaited, I see. I suppose it's too much to ask for too many miracles in one go.'

Carolyn did her best not to cringe away from his hands on her flesh. She knew they weren't really sexual hands. Or sexual words. Only mocking, teasing ones. And she steadfastly refused to give him the satisfaction of rising to his bait.

When he turned her back to face him, his expression was drily amused. 'But be warned. Any further improvements and I might be forced to make a pass at you.'

Now her temper flared. Who did he think he was, turning her this way and that, mocking her all the while? 'If you would prefer,' she snapped, 'I'll dress in neck-to-knee all the time in future. I'd hate to put your male ego through the unnecessary strain of having to make a pass at a woman who's bitter and twisted.'

His fingers tightened, nails digging slightly into her flesh. She looked up to see his eyes darken and flash. 'God, I'd like to——'

'What?' she cut in with cold challenge, though her heart was pounding so loudly she was sure he must hear it. 'Show me I'm right about you? Prove that you're nothing but a callous seducer, that you've never wanted a woman for any other reason than *just sex*?'

His hands dropped from her as though stung, his eyes wide.

Dismay clutched at Carolyn's stomach as she realised she had once again allowed this to happen. No wonder Vaughan was looking at her at this very moment in such an appalled fashion. She kept on over-reacting to him, taunting him as he unwittingly taunted her with his overt sexuality. Even now, she couldn't take her eyes off his bare chest. She wanted to touch it, oh so badly. She wanted . . .

The memory of seeing his bare chest another time, ten years ago, blasted back to her mind. Only it wasn't her own hands she pictured running over his muscles with mindless passion. It was another pair of hands, the hands of a woman who'd been destroyed by the owner of that bare chest.

A sob was torn from Carolyn's heart, a sob of utter despair. She whirled away from Vaughan's startled face to cover her own with her hands. Shame curdled through her insides. More sobs punched from her throat.

When tender fingers curved gently over her shoulders again she tried to pull away but he would have none of it, tightening his grasp and easing her firmly back against him, arms sliding forward to wrap around her chest.

'Don't,' Vaughan groaned. 'For God's sake, don't. It's all right...really. *I* started it with my stupid remarks. I'm sorry...I didn't mean to upset you. It's just that you...you get under my skin.'

Her sobs were choked off by the awful reality of his crushing and very intimate embrace. She could feel his thighs, hard behind hers, his breath warm in her hair, his heart beating against her back. She could feel far too much of him.

'No, you've *got* under my skin,' he rasped, his lips moving across her hair, dropping down to brush over one ear.

A shiver of sheer electric pleasure ran down her spine. For a second, she succumbed to the temptation of melting back into him, but when she felt his flesh stir against her buttocks she was truly shocked.

'I haven't been able to stop thinking about you for two weeks. I want you, Carolyn, in a way I've never wanted a woman before. I——'

She wrenched out of his arms and away from him, spinning round with horror in her eyes at the way he had made her feel. So quickly and so easily. Within a hair's breadth of surrender.

'No!' she screamed. 'No! You...you keep away from me. Don't touch me. I hate you!'

'Do you?' he ground out, harsh eyes taking in the uncontrollable tremors that had begun to wrack her body. 'I don't think so, Carolyn. Not even remotely. You're fighting what's been growing between us because of your mother. You mistakenly think she'd care if——'

Maddie's black car accelerated around the corner up the road and into view. Vaughan swore. 'Of all the wrong damned moments.'

'The *right* damned moment,' Carolyn flung back at him, shaking hands smoothing several escaping strands of hair away from her flushed face.

'We'll finish this discussion later, madam,' he said with steely resolve. 'When we won't be interrupted. Meanwhile, I suggest you try to look less like a girl who's just been ravished. Unless of course you want Maddie to know the truth about us. For my own part, I don't give a damn who knows how I feel about you!'

'There is no *us*!' she cried.

His eyes were merciless. 'Yes, there bloody well is. And one day I'm going to make you admit it!'

'Over my dead body!'

'Oh, no, Carolyn,' he vowed darkly. 'Over your very *alive* body.'

Maddie's car scattered gravel as it ground to a halt. She bounded from behind the wheel, an individualistic picture in a black cotton jumpsuit with bright red hibiscus flowers embroidered on it, a V neckline cut lower than the defence budget and slits halfway up each leg which flapped wildly as she walked, showing long slender legs. Indian-style red sandals graced her feet. Huge red flower ear-rings swung from her ears.

'Yes, I know it's me who's late this time,' she greeted, smiling broadly. 'But it wasn't my fault. Mrs Makepiece just couldn't make up her mind what fabric she wanted for the bedroom curtains, the poor indecisive darling. Don't worry, Vaughan, I steered her gently in the right direction. Well, if it isn't Carolyn, looking divinely cool and gorgeous! God, it's hot!' She scowled at Vaughan's bare chest. 'Haven't you ever heard of skin cancer? You should be wearing a T-shirt at this time of day.'

'But of course,' he returned drily. 'I've noticed how covered up *you* are.'

'I have my factor fifteen sun-screen all over my beautiful body. Speaking of beautiful bodies, I hope you've been leaving Carolyn's alone, you bad boy. She looks a little rattled. I'll tell Anthea if you haven't.'

Now it was Vaughan's turn to scowl. 'I don't give a stuff what you tell Anthea!' And he stormed off towards the house.

Maddie rolled her eyes. 'My, but he *is* in a good mood today.' She walked over and linked arms with Carolyn. 'He's been like that for a couple of weeks. Perhaps he and Anthea have had a tiff. You know what men like Vaughan are like when they're not having their regular dose of sex. *Very* liverish. Oh, well, at least *we* know not to get tangled up with him, don't we? Come on, let's go and see how the edifice is looking before cranky-pants starts smashing the walls in with his chin.'

Carolyn tried not to laugh. Truly, she should have been shattered, not amused. But once they met up with Vaughan again she saw that his chin *was* jutting out like that of a two-year-old boy about to throw a tantrum. Not only that, he had dragged a T-shirt over his naked torso which had written on it, 'I Used To Be A Masochist. Now I Just Build Houses!'

She took one look at him and started to giggle, the giggles soon dissolving into outright laughter. For a few seconds, he looked affronted, but then a wide grin split his face and he too laughed.

'Methinks I've missed something here,' Maddie frowned, looking from one to the other and perhaps detecting a slightly black edge to their amusement.

But then Vaughan did something that stunned Carolyn. He walked over and kissed her. Only a light lingering of lips, but she was too surprised to do a thing but stand there and let him. When his head lifted he lanced her with a wry, almost self-mocking look.

'Truce?' he said softly.

She nodded dumbly.

'I've *definitely* missed something,' Maddie intoned drily.

'A kiss of peace, Maddie,' he drawled. 'That's all. We had a little difference of opinion before you arrived.'

'Oh, yes? What about?'

'Nothing important,' Carolyn jumped in, which brought an approving look from Vaughan.

'In that case, can we get on with this tour of duty?' Maddie asked. 'I have an important date tonight and I have an appointment at the hairdresser's in less than an hour.'

'God, not another man, Maddie,' Vaughan groaned.

'It's only a *date*,' she countered. 'Anyway, do I make judgements about your sex life? Don't make any about mine!'

Half an hour later she was gone, and Carolyn was once again alone with Vaughan. He slanted her an almost watchful look and immediately every instinctive nerve in her body screamed at her to get away from here—and him—as quickly as possible.

'I . . . I must be going too,' she said.

'*Must* you?' A faint mocking tone was back in his voice.

'Yes.' There was a finality in the word that wasn't in her heart. She wanted to stay. Terribly.

He shrugged, irritation in the action. 'What about that swim we were going to have?' He strolled over to where she was standing by the newly filled and filtered pool.

'Go on,' he urged. 'Go and get your cossie. The water's great. It'll cool you down before your long drive home.'

Before she could say another word, he whisked his T-shirt over his head and stepped out of his shorts. Carolyn tried not to stare at the way his brief white trunks clung. But stare she did. He noticed her avid attention too, a surprised though decidedly pleased sparkle in his eyes before he turned away and dived gracefully into the pool.

What to do? she agonised.

Common sense told her to walk away, to get into the BMW and just drive off. But some dark tempting voice kept whispering to do what he asked, to go and put on her costume, to stay and have that swim.

He surfaced, flicking his head so that a shower of droplets sprayed around him. His hands lifted to smooth back the sides of his hair and he frowned at her. 'Haven't you gone to get your things yet?'

'No... Yes... I mean... Vaughan, I don't think I should.'

He swam over and levered himself out of the pool, picking up a nearby towel and walking slowly towards her, wiping his face. But his eyes never left hers.

He dropped the towel when he reached her, and quite slowly and deliberately pulled her into his arms. Stunned, she offered no resistance, but her eyes grew wide at the feel of his damp, hard body pressed against hers. 'Do you *want* to stay?' he asked in a husky voice.

She blinked and opened her mouth to say something but nothing came out. Her mind was no longer connected to her tongue.

For a few seconds longer he stared down at her. 'Let's see if I can't help you make up your mind...' And his mouth slowly descended.

How long later did it lift again? A minute? Two?

Carolyn had no idea, for instantly those soft sensual lips claimed hers she was catapulted into a world so erotic and exciting that all coherent thought rocketed to a distant planet. She clung to him, her lips parting soundlessly beneath the increasing pressure of his, letting his tongue slide forward into her mouth, letting him arouse her with it to a pitch she would never have believed possible from a kiss. The blood began swimming in her head and wave upon wave of heat flooded up through her body. When her knees threatened to buckle from under her, she slid her arms up tightly around his neck, her small hard breasts pressed flat against his wet chest. But when a low moan murmured in her throat, the kiss was abruptly terminated.

Dazed eyes opened to see Vaughan wasn't much more controlled than herself, his eyes glittering, his breathing heavy. 'God, Carolyn,' he rasped, clearly in a type of shock at her unbridled response.

'Don't stop,' she whispered shakily, and sank back into him.

He groaned, his head dipping to take her mouth once more, firing her blood further, taking her one step closer to the point of no return. But once again, it was Vaughan who terminated the kiss, drawing back to hold her at arm's length.

'I think we both need to cool down a little,' he said in a desire-thickened voice. 'Or I might end up doing something *you'll* undoubtedly regret later. Your body wants me, Carolyn, but your mind needs a little more time before it wants me too. When that happens—and it will—you won't have a hope in Hades of stopping me, sweetheart. You have my word on that! Now be a good girl and get that cossie of yours on,' he said as he spun her round and tapped her on the bottom. 'I've a mind to see you in far less than you've got on at this moment.'

And so doing, he dived back into the pool and stroked steadily away from her. For a moment she just stood there, her mind whirling as she tried to grasp what had just happened, what was *going* to happen between herself and this man. But her dangerously aroused body would have none of reason and soon she was turning on robotic legs and making her way out to the BMW. Once there, she opened the passenger door and drew out the beach-bag that contained her things, shivering as she thought about how accessible her body would be in such a thin, scanty garment.

Slowly, the cogs of reason began to slide back into gear.

There was no point in pretending she didn't know what would happen once she was half-naked in the pool with Vaughan. A man like him—so carnal, despite his noble words—would not be able to help himself. Already in her mind's eyes he was kissing her again, touching her all over, peeling the costume away from her already swollen breasts, bending that hot, fiery mouth to the rock-hard tips, sucking on them, licking them.

Carolyn—whose breasts had never been *seen* let alone suckled by a man—swayed with the shock of her mental images, of her bold desires. For she wanted to bend her mouth to him also, to taste his flesh, to...

The explicit and quite shocking nature of her fantasies brought her up with a jolt.

I *can't* let any of this happen, she groaned. No matter what my body feels and wants, Vaughan is the one man in the entire world I must not become involved with, for to do so would be to risk a relationship far more important to me than a sexual fling. That of mother and daughter.

But to say no, to walk away from such pleasure...

She moaned, shocked by the real pain of thwarted desire. It made her realise how strong lust could be. How awfully, awfully strong. It was there, in every tightly strung muscle, in every charged nerve-ending, tempting her, begging her to give in.

Carolyn would never have dreamt that she was capable of wanting a relationship that was 'just sex'. But she had to accept that where the pleasures of the flesh were concerned, she was as weak as the next person. Even now, she wanted to go back to Vaughan, to strip herself totally naked in front of him, to tell him to do whatever he willed with her.

Gathering every mental resource she had, Carolyn began to fight the cruel temptations with desperate logic. Surely one day, there'll be another man for me. Another man who'll make me feel like this, another man whom I'll love as well as lust after, another man who won't be such a bastard.

It worked, her intense desire subsiding and her mind clearing till she could focus much more coldly and angrily on the man she'd just been contemplating taking as her first lover. How *dared* he start seducing her, when he was already having an affair with Anthea Maxwell? And how dared he think he could move from mother to daughter without batting an eyelash. Her mother wouldn't mind, he'd said. What a laugh! The man had no conscience when it came to women and sex!

But my God, she'd almost fallen right into his insatiable lap with a few smoothly delivered lines, a few measly kisses. How pathetic could she get? And how pathetic was he, waiting smugly for her to join him, arrogant in his prediction that she would eventually become his?

Dropping her things back into the car, Carolyn lifted her chin and strode determinedly back to the concrete courtyard and the side of the pool. She stood by the edge, arms folded, head held high. Vaughan saw her, stopped swimming and looked up. His eyes narrowed when he encountered her stance and the stony mask she'd pulled down over her recently aroused face.

'Let me guess,' he drawled bitterly. 'You've changed your mind about joining me.'

'That's right,' she bit out. 'And I think you know why. I'm only glad I came to my senses in time. I suggest you go back to bedding widows, Vaughan. They might be able to handle your brand of sexual conduct. I know I never could.'

Face tight and hard, he stood up in the water like an angry Neptune, water streaming from his beautiful bronzed body. 'I haven't been bedding widows. Not since I met you. Now stop being a silly ninny,' he growled, 'and get yourself into this pool. This is the wrong weather to be playing games.'

When she didn't move a muscle—she'd been frozen by the sight of his almost naked wet body— he made an impatient sound and began moving purposefully across to the steps at the shallow end of the pool. Panic seized Carolyn at the thought that he was going to try to physically persuade her stay. Knowing that he probably could, she whirled and started running.

He caught her at the car, spinning her round and slamming her against the door. 'Why are you doing this, Carolyn? *Why*? Is this some sort of revenge? To torment me with glimpses of the real you, the very desirable real you... To whet my appetite, inflame my desire, then run away, leaving me in torment.'

'You're mad!' she flung back at him, all the while trying to twist her face out of his iron grasp. 'I . . . I haven't been doing any such thing.'

'Haven't you? Well, in that case what I keep seeing and feeling must be the genuine article. Shall we test it? Shall we see if Carolyn's desire is a ploy, or the real McCoy?'

'No, *don't*!'

Her struggles against him were stupid, his water-slicked body rubbing against hers, sending a thousand messages along her nerve-endings to her brain. She felt her nipples harden betrayingly, felt a flood of warmth and desire between her thighs.

'No,' she groaned again only a breath before his mouth took hers.

His lips were hard—brutal even—clamping on to hers and dragging them open to give his tongue full reign within her mouth. Never had Carolyn been kissed like this. So cruelly and savagely. His tongue plunged again and again, his hands holding her face captive beneath the onslaught. There was no real pleasure for her, only whirlpools of wild sensation whipping around and around in her head. She began to whimper with distress and when Vaughan suddenly yanked back from her, she sank, semi-conscious, to the ground beside the car.

'Oh, God,' she heard him groan as he scooped her up and cradled her against his damp body. Lifting her high in his arms, he carried her back to the poolside and lay her gently down along the edge, then dipped his hand in the water to wipe a cool wet palm over her face. 'Carolyn, open your eyes. Say something. For God's sake, just say something.'

Her eyes stayed shut but two large tears trickled from their corners down the sides of her face. 'Don't,' she sobbed. 'Just don't . . .' And she rolled away from him and drew her legs up into a tight little ball of misery.

'I won't,' he assured her, his voice bleak. 'Believe me, I won't. I . . . I don't know what came over me. I've never acted like that with a woman in my whole life.'

Because you've never needed to, Carolyn thought wretchedly as she lay there, curled up in the foetal position. There's never been a woman who's said no to you. And if I stay here with you now, there never will be.

For even his brutal kiss had aroused her unbearably, had left her aching for him.

Slowly she uncurled herself and sat up. 'I . . . I must go home.'

'You can't drive all the way back to Sydney the way you are now!' he said, horrified.

'Yes, I can. I *have* to.'

'Carolyn, be sensible . . .'

'I am being sensible,' she said in a cold, flat voice, but without looking his way. She knew she shouldn't have stayed in the first place, yet she had. Now she had to remove herself from any further temptation. And quickly.

'Please don't worry about me,' she went on, getting to her feet. 'I've been responsible for myself for a long time. I'm not going to do anything stupid. I'll be fine.'

'Yes,' he muttered. 'Yes, I'm sure you will be. You *are* a very strong, sensible girl.'

Now she did turn on him, a bitter laugh escaping her lips. 'No, I'm not,' she denied vehemently. 'I'm a stupid, weak girl. And do you know why? Because I *do* want you. In every crude way possible. Which is quite laughable. Because I'm a virgin, a prissy uptight little fool who thought she'd save herself for the man she loved, yet here I am lusting after a man who's had so many women he's probably lost count. How's that for stupid and weak!'

His face twisted with true anguish. 'Carolyn, I——' He reached out a hand.

'Don't touch me!' she screamed, and knocked his hand away. 'Don't ever touch me again. If you do, I . . . I'll kill you!'

He stepped back from her, truly shocked. 'You don't mean that.'

'Try me.' She clenched her teeth hard in her jaw.

He shook his head. 'You're distraught.'

'Too damned right I am.'

'You shouldn't be allowed to drive. Let me call Maddie.'

'Maddie's getting ready to go out. And I . . . am . . . fine,' she bit out. 'Now move aside and let me go. And don't ring me again, either. I'll deal with Maddie in future.'

He moved to stand in front of her, his face hardening. 'You're wrong about me, Carolyn. I haven't had that many women. And you're wrong about yourself. This isn't just lust between us. There's something more . . .'

She laughed. 'Maybe. Maybe not. But even if you were right, it wouldn't make any difference.

Because the point is, there's been one too many women in your life, Vaughan. One too many...'

And with that, she pushed him aside and strode off.

This time he didn't come after her.

CHAPTER SEVEN

THE next month was the worst time of Carolyn's life. Not even the ghastly days after her mother's breakdown could rival the inner despair and distress she felt fighting this awful attraction for a man she couldn't—or shouldn't—have. Worst was the knowledge that she only had to lift the phone and ring him, apologise, confess she wanted him like crazy, and he would probably be on her doorstep before one could say 'Jack Robinson'. Vaughan Slater was not backward in coming forward where willing women were concerned.

How many times did her hand hover over the receiver, her heart beating madly, her emotions in turmoil? How many disgusting reasons did she come up with to rationalise actually doing such a dreadful thing?

It's not such a big deal... Everyone's doing it these days... It's not as though you want to *marry* him... Your mother need never find out... A brief affair and this fever will probably burn itself out...

Thank God she always found the courage to snatch back her hand, to turn her back on those wickedly seductive arguments.

Though she suffered for it. Not sleeping well, then stuffing herself with chocolates and all sorts of fattening takeaway food. She felt even worse when the people at work started telling her how well she was looking with the added weight. My God, she even acquired a quite enviable *bust*, which was hardly what she had in mind.

In the end, she controlled her eating binges and started exercising furiously, but her extra curves remained, her newly lush breasts and shapely bottom mocking her every day in the bathroom by their visible sensuality. Some of her underwear didn't even fit her any more.

When she was finally forced to purchase some new bras, Carolyn found herself gravitating towards the lacy half-cup variety which gave her a cleavage for the first time in her life. Feeling guilty but oddly excited, she lashed out on a couple of sexy black ones, her guilt increasing when she gave in to the saleswoman's pressure to buy matching bikini panties, the ones that were extra high-cut with lace inserts that left nothing to the imagination.

She went home from shopping that night, knowing that she hadn't bought the erotic underwear for her upfront sensible self. She had bought it for that wicked secret part that still longed to call Vaughan, that dreamed of how it would feel to have his hot brown eyes on her as he undressed her with excruciating slowness, that ached to have his body move over and into hers.

Outwardly, she dressed no differently for work. But she was always hotly aware that underneath, her flesh was contained within sheer lacy nothingnesses, and more than once she found herself flushing with a sexual awareness that both stirred and appalled her.

At times like these she felt grateful for her decision not to go down to inspect the house any more. For heaven alone knew how she'd cope with being that close to Vaughan's disturbing physical presence. Dreaming about him every night was bad enough. But to see him again in the flesh ...

Maddie had not sounded convinced over the phone that Carolyn was too busy to make the trip every weekend, or that she was more than happy to leave all the decisions up to her. But a good businesswoman could hardly argue with a client. Maddie had said, however, that she would expect Carolyn to come down and check over the furniture when it arrived in five or six weeks' time, to which she reluctantly agreed.

Meanwhile, each day passed very slowly.

On the Friday afternoon of the fourth week after her poolside encounter with Vaughan, Carolyn was alone in the office copying room, xeroxing some documents, her mind in a blank daze with fatigue from not sleeping well the night before, when a hand suddenly curved suggestively over her bottom. Gasping, she spun round, only to encounter Maurice Jenkins looking at her with a decidedly lascivious expression on his face.

'Do you *mind*?' she snapped.

The doctor smiled and remained standing in front of her, spreading his arms on either side of the copier so that she was effectively imprisoned. 'Come on, Carolyn,' he drawled. 'I realise modern young ladies are expected to act affronted when a guy makes a pass at them, but underneath we both know you don't mind. I've been quietly watching you, honey, and you'd have to be the sexiest thing on two legs in this hospital. I've no idea how I didn't notice before.'

His smile widened smugly. 'Besides, I was talking to one of your workmates yesterday and she told me that BMW you're driving around belongs to your new rich stepdaddy who's overseas on his honeymoon. So I said to myself, why did Carolyn imply to me the other week that she'd spent a hot weekend with some wealthy boyfriend? The only logical answer was that she wanted me to know she liked being shown a good time, that she was available for some fun and games with the right sort of man.'

His arms started sliding up her arms. 'Well, here I am, honey,' he murmured thickly. 'Ready, willing and able. Just tell me where you'd like me to start. Here?' One hand lifted to brush over her stunned mouth. 'Or maybe here...?' Both hands covered her breasts, thumbs rubbing over her nipples through the material of her blouse and bra.

Carolyn actually thought she was going to be sick. But within seconds she recognised her stomach churning as blind rage rising within her. With a strength born of anger and adrenalin, she pushed the doctor away, then swung her whole arm in a wide circle, her open palm cracking him a vicious blow across the face.

'You bitch!' he gasped, holding a trembling hand against the red welt on his cheek. 'I'll have you fired for this. Not only fired! I...I'll...'

'Oh, put a sock in it, creep!' she said contemptuously. 'I quit anyway.' And with that she gave him another shove, sending him sprawling into the corner in a most ungainly heap. 'You should know better than to tangle with a McKensie!' she pronounced, and marched indignantly from the room.

She did quit. On the spot, and without an ounce of real regret, only then realising how bored she'd been in her job for some time. She was fed up with filling in forms, doing endless paperwork, filing, typing, answering the telephone. Vaughan had been right in that regard. She had been a bright student at school and really needed something more to challenge her natural intelligence than routine office work.

Carolyn reasoned that now her mother was no longer a financial burden she could take some time finding another job, maybe even another career.

Yet as she emptied her desk and saw all the sad faces around her, Carolyn did feel a momentary regret. She'd come to know all her workmates very well over the years. Their company had filled a large chunk of her life. She would miss them.

Of course she hadn't been allowed to walk out without a confrontation with Matron and the administration head, who demanded to know the real truth behind her hasty resignation. She told them. In no uncertain terms.

They weren't surprised. They were even sympathetic and apologetic. But they didn't try too hard to persuade her to stay. Neither did they suggest that Dr Jenkins would be disciplined in any way. There was certainly no suggestion that *he* might be asked to leave instead of her. The world didn't work that way.

By the time Carolyn made it out to the BMW shortly after four o'clock, doubt and depression had begun to take hold. Maybe she *had* been hasty in quitting so precipitately. Now she didn't even have a job to distract her from thinking about Vaughan,

and there were three weeks to go till her mother
and Julian arrived back from Europe.

As well as that, on the drive back to Ashfield,
the radio programme she switched on started dis-
cussing the appalling state of unemployment, and
Carolyn realised she might not find another job all
that quickly. OK, so she had some savings. But not
all that much. And from now on she would have
to pay for the whole rent of the flat herself. Her
mother's contribution from her pension would be
a thing of the past.

The sight of a couple of overseas postcards
sticking out of her letter-box cheered her up enormously. They weren't the first she had received,
others having come from London and Amsterdam
and Cologne. But she really needed to hear from
her mother today, needed to feel loved and
remembered.

Her spirits revived, she pulled them out of the
box, staring delightedly at the pictures of Paris as
she hurried up the flight of stairs to her door. Once
inside, she threw the rest of her things down on a
chair and flopped on to the sofa, turning over the
Eiffel Tower to read what her mother had written
on the other side.

Darling, Having a marvellous time. Paris is so
romantic! I've bought you some perfume and a
few other goodies I hope you'll like. Missing you
terribly. Julian has some good news for you. At
least, *I* think it's good. I hope you do too. Please
don't say no! It's what we both want. Lots of
love and kisses, Mum.

Tears pricked at Carolyn's eyes.

Mum sounds so happy, she thought with real joy. But what is this good news she talks about?

Julian's much larger card was flipped over eagerly.

My dear Carolyn. You'll never guess what I've done. I've told Isabel about the house! I just couldn't keep it to myself last night. We'd had a few glasses of champagne and were telling each other all our deep dark secrets—as tipsy people do—and I just blurted it out! Aren't I a duffer? Anyway, Isabel was thrilled to bits, though once I'd explained where the house was and how far from Ashfield her lovely face fell. What about my Carolyn? she cried. I'll never see her! She can come and live with us, I said. Well, I've never seen my darling so radiant. She was beside herself. So I promised to make you quit that dreary job of yours and come live with us in Wollongong. Don't worry about getting another job. I have so many connections down the south coast you won't have any trouble. So if you're in agreement—as I feel sure you will be—put in your resignation, give the estate agent your notice to quit the flat and start packing!

Actually, you're welcome to move in to the new house as soon as it's habitable, which, if things are on schedule, should be at the end of next week. Quite frankly, it would be good for security if you did. Hate to come home and find the stove and microwave missing. Now don't let that very conservative nature of yours get in the way of all these great new plans. They won't miss you at the hospital. No one's indispensable, you know. Though I think you might be to your mother's happiness! Now don't quibble. Do something crazy and carefree for once. See you first week in April. Your loving step-papa, Julian.

A whole array of emotions coursed through Carolyn as she read the letter. Joy...she would like nothing better than to live with her Mother and Julian in that beautiful home. Relief...she no longer had to worry about a job, or the rent of the flat.

But alongside the joy and relief was dismay. Wollongong was where Vaughan lived...

And then came a panicky confusion. If Julian had told Isabel about the house, wouldn't he have mentioned Vaughan's name? If he had, surely her mother *wouldn't* have sounded so happy...

Of course, she finally sighed with grim understanding. Julian *hadn't* mentioned Vaughan's name.

Yet.

He hadn't when talking with herself about the house either, just calling Vaughan 'the architect', or merely 'he'. Her mother obviously had no idea who the designer of her new home was. But for how long would that situation last? Perhaps, if Carolyn was lucky, Isabel wouldn't find out, and as soon as they got home she'd whisper some very clever white lies in Julian's ear to avoid disaster.

What clever white lies? she groaned.

Carolyn was mulling over the sort of plausible story she could invent when her telephone rang. Immediately, her nerves were on full alert. She rarely got phone calls. And the last time it had been Vaughan...

Rather reluctantly she stood up and walked over to the telephone table, staring down at the receiver for a second before snatching it up as if it were a snake about to strike.

'Yes?' she said abruptly.

'Dear me,' Maddie sighed. 'You're in no better mood than Vaughan by the sound of you!'

'Maddie!' Carolyn said with smiling relief.

'Now that's better. Makes me almost glad I rang you.'

'Why *are* you ringing me?' Carolyn asked. 'Did the furniture come earlier than you expected?'

'Huh! Not likely. Though we did lay the carpet and slate this week and put in all the light fittings. So there is something for you to see if you would like to change your mind and come down. Not only that, I'm having a few people over tomorrow night for drinks and a bit of a shindig, and I'm always on the lookout for new blood and thought of you. Would you like to come?'

Carolyn's heart jumped. 'Yes, I would,' she admitted. Then added, 'But not if Vaughan's going to be there.'

'Mr Anti-Party? Good God, he's never graced one of *my* dos in all the years I've known him. I always ask, just to see what new excuse he can come up with not to come. Do you know what it is this time? He has to work. Now isn't that original! No, dear heart, you're safe from the clutches of the evil warlord of architecture. He's not on the rampage this weekend. So what do you say? You can sleep

the night at my place. That way you can have a few
little drinkies.'

Carolyn laughed. Maddie was so good for her
spirits! 'You've talked me into it.'

'Good. Shall we say noon at the house?'

'Isn't noon a bit early? We'll be finished by one
and then you'll have to put up with me for the rest
of the afternoon.'

'Oh, don't worry about that?' Maddie said airily.
'I'll think of something for us to do. See you
tomorrow, then. And bring something snazzy to
wear for the evening. My parties are definitely not
attended by the jeans and T-shirt set. See you. Bye!'

She rang off abruptly, leaving Carolyn dithering
over what she should bring to wear. In the end, she
dismissed worrying about it. Since Vaughan wasn't
going to be there, feasting on her with mocking yet
hungry eyes, she figured she could just about wear
anything, even the form-hugging red sheath she'd
worn to Isabel's wedding. After all, whatever she
wore would look tame next to Maddie's no doubt
outrageous outfit.

Saturday dawned cloudy in Sydney but as
Carolyn drove southwards the clouds dissipated and
the sun appeared, bathing the coastline in a mild
March heat. Maddie was waiting for her at the
house, even though she wasn't late, and they were
through their inspecting by twelve-thirty.

'It's going to be a fantastic house,' Carolyn complimented as they walked together back to their
cars.

'Yes. Vaughan's outdone himself this time. Not
that every one of his houses isn't special. But this
is...more special, I think. Of course, he liked Julian

enormously, and that always makes you want to do better for the client.'

'Julian's a terrific man,' Carolyn agreed. 'But it's not just Vaughan whose work is wonderful. You're pretty good yourself, Maddie. Those old brass colonial light fittings look great. Yet the rest of the place is either modern or faintly European. I would never have thought such a range of styles could be blended so successfully. But you've managed it to perfection.'

'Yes, I thought so too,' she preened without sounding at all vain.

'I'm going to enjoy living in it,' Carolyn said, and waited, smiling, for all Maddie's inevitable questions. They came in a rush.

'But that's simply marvellous!' the other woman enthused finally. 'Now we can really become friends with your living so close. I'll help you move in as soon as the furniture comes. And if you get desperate for a job, you can work for me as my receptionist. I'm doing well enough to hire a permanent one now. I've been making do with temps.'

Carolyn hesitated.

Intuitive Maddie needed no further explanation. 'Aah . . . Too close to the dreaded Vaughan.' She sighed. 'One of these days, you'll have to tell me what went on there. If you don't I'm going to die of curiosity.'

Carolyn laughed. 'I can't imagine you dying of anything.'

'No? Boredom might do me in. I can't stand not being busy. So! Are you going to do what I asked or not?'

'What was that?' If she meant tell her about Vaughan, then she would have to be disappointed. As much as Carolyn valued her growing friendship with this way-out, wonderfully warm lady, she wasn't ready for such confidences yet. Perhaps one day...

'Why, pose for that painting, of course!' Maddie said exasperatedly. 'You must have known I'd ask again sooner or later, and we have plenty of time to get started this afternoon. The light's good and you're looking...' Her sharp eyes ran over Carolyn again, dressed at that moment in loose white cotton pants and a colourful blouse which flowed out over her hips. A dark frown settled on Maddie's vibrant face.

'Carolyn,' she said in a low, troubled voice, 'you're not pregnant, are you? You and Vaughan didn't—er...?' She wriggled her black winged eyebrows and expressive hands in a suggestive fashion.

'No!' came her indignant but slightly guilty denial. There but for the grace of God... 'But I have been eating like a little piggy lately,' she confessed on a groan. 'I guess I'm lonely with Mum away so long. Do I look terrible?'

'Far from it. You have more up here...' Hands waved across her chest. 'And here...' Maddie patted her own bottom. 'Which is great, since I'd like to paint a rear view.'

'A *rear* view?'

'Oh, yes, men find that *very* erotic. And men buy my nudes. I won't have any trouble selling your painting, believe me, and you won't mind because no one'll ever know it's you!'

'Yes, but...'

'I'll pay you, of course. Standard model's fees.'

'It's not the money, Maddie. I'm just not sure I'd be able to take my clothes off and stand there like that in——'

'*Lie*,' Maddie interrupted briskly.

Carolyn blinked her confusion.

'You'll be lying down. On your side. On a red satin sheet,' she added with a gleeful smile and a little shiver of obvious delight. 'With your hair all spread out. Oooh, it gives me goose-bumps just thinking about how smashing it's going to be. My best yet, I'll warrant. I'll sell it for a mint. Go on, please say you'll do it. Please, please, pretty please.'

Carolyn's first instinct was still to refuse. But Maddie put such a doleful appealing look into her eyes, she just couldn't.

She shook her head, a rueful smile on her face. 'All right. You've conned me into it. But no payment, please. I'm doing this as a gesture of friendship. Though, believe me, there will be *no* repeat performances from the front!'

'Agreed! Now follow me closely. Can't have my most exciting model to date getting lost.'

Maddie's place was an old weatherboard house which had been startlingly refurbished in Maddie's inimitable personal style of clear bright colours and more than a healthy dose of black. If anyone had told Carolyn that a black and red bathroom could look terrific she would have thought them mad. But it did! Or, at least, it did in Maddie's house. By the time she'd finished the grand tour, however, Carolyn was glad that Maddie watered down her personal taste when it came to other people's homes.

Once she'd made the necessary complimentary comments about the décor, Carolyn was ushered through to the back of the house where a glassed-in veranda had been converted into an artist's studio. The beach lay less than fifty metres from the back door and the light was, indeed, excellent.

Carolyn gulped when her eyes moved to the bed-like divan that lay across one end of the veranda. No doubt this was where she would be lying. She tried to picture it covered with red satin and herself spread out in a seductive pose for a couple of hours, totally nude. Her stomach churned and she gnawed nervously at her bottom lip. Why on earth had she agreed?

'We'll have a spot of lunch first,' Maddie announced brightly. 'And then we'll get to work.'

Strangely enough, Carolyn didn't have as much trouble stripping off as she thought she would have. When it came to models, Maddie was all professional, treating Carolyn and her body with the impersonality of a doctor. Though she did leave a bath-robe for Carolyn within easy reach. And of course, it was a lot easier having any scrutinising eyes behind her, rather than gazing at her full frontal nudity.

Once Maddie had posed Carolyn into the position she wanted—one arm stretched up under her head, the other draped over her hip, her hair out in full—she retreated to work in silence, leaving Carolyn to close her eyes and relax. There was no point in keeping them open, since she was looking at a blank, black-papered wall. After a good while Carolyn found herself on the edge of sleep. She possibly would have drifted right off, if Maddie hadn't spoken up.

'Have you told Vaughan the news about your moving into the house?' she asked. 'No, don't *move*! Damn. Look forget I said that. Stupid of me. You've gone all tight in the shoulders. Just relax again, will you? We'll talk about Vaughan later. Think of something pleasant instead, something soft and dreamy...'

Carolyn did her level best. And she must have succeeded. On the surface. Since Maddie didn't complain further.

But if her exterior seemed relaxed, her interior certainly wasn't.

Having Vaughan catapulted back into her mind like that exhumed all the worrying possibilities that the move to Wollongong would bring. But Maddie was right. Vaughan would have to be informed about Julian giving her permission to move into his house before his return. And informed soon.

The prospect of meeting with Vaughan again was daunting in the extreme.

The only consolation to her rapidly knotting insides was that time might have cured Vaughan's interest in her. Maybe he'd even resumed relations with Anthea Maxwell. For despite his protest that he felt more for her than desire, Carolyn was convinced his feelings had only been a mixture of sex and ego—he probably found her resistance challenging. Nothing more. They didn't know each other well enough for anything deeper. What little they did know, they didn't even like!

It had taken Carolyn quite some time, however, to accept her brush with lust for what it was. But she finally had, along with all its subsequently ambivalent feelings. She now accepted that, while she didn't admire the feelings Vaughan evoked in her, they were still very real feelings, with very real consequences, very real powers. How else could she explain her sudden pleasure in wearing sexy underclothes? Or the heated arousal in her body when she awoke from one of the many lurid dreams that plagued her at night?

There was no denying she could experience revulsion and excitement side by side. Self-disgust, along with the most incredible temptation. It was a constant battle, between what she knew was right . . . and what she so desperately wanted . . .

To have Vaughan look at her once more with desire. To have him touch her again. Kiss her again. To have him do all those things to her she'd only ever read about, and which had previously made her cringe with embarrassment.

Carolyn suppressed a groan and literally willed the explicit images from her mind. If he had been any other man, she agonised, she might have given in to her baser side, might have indulged her flesh with the sort of wild abandon she suspected lay within her virginal body. Without love. Without strings.

But this wasn't any other man. This was Vaughan Slater. Which meant that love and strings were already involved. Not hers. Her mother's.

Don't forget that, Carolyn, the voice of conscience reminded her. For if you do, you'll regret it for the rest of your life!

I won't, she vowed. I won't.

And with several deep, slow, steadying breaths she closed her eyes again and let a soothing blankness wash over her, calming her heartbeat, cooling the flush that had come over her skin with her earlier thoughts.

An hour of relative peace ticked away, the only sounds Maddie's occasional grunt or mutter. Carolyn was relatively relaxed when, all of a sudden, a prickling seized the back of her neck, the sort of sensation one got when certain one was being surreptitiously watched. Carolyn tried telling herself she was being paranoid because she'd never lain around in broad daylight in the nude before. It was probably only Maddie's gaze, concentrating hard to visually capture a difficult line, or curve, *Maddie's* black eyes that she could feel boring into the back of her head, travelling slowly down her spine, lingering on the swell of her bottom.

But Carolyn didn't think so. Nothing could shake the suspicion that hot *male* eyes were devouring her at that very moment.

It was very disturbing. Her breath began coming in short shallow pants. A fine sheen of sweat broke out on her skin. The temptation to swing round and look over her shoulder was excruciatingly strong. Yet she couldn't bring herself to do it. The seconds ticked away, with agonising slowness. She couldn't stand the tension much longer. She just couldn't!

'For God's sake!' Maddie groaned when Carolyn abruptly sat up and grabbed the robe, clutching it over her bare body as she swung around, blue eyes wide. They flashed straight to the high wide windows and ran the full length of the veranda.

No one was there. Not a single solitary soul. Carolyn frowned. There wasn't even a suitable window nearby for anyone to be peering at her through binoculars.

Maddie put down her brush with a resigned sigh. 'I presume that's it for the day?'

'I . . . I thought someone was watching me.'

Maddie frowned and glanced around. 'As you can see, you were wrong.'

'Yes . . .' But her heart was still beating madly. 'Yes, I suppose so,' she agreed reluctantly.

'Would you like to see what I've done so far?'

Carolyn dragged on the bathrobe and stood up. 'Yes, I would.'

She was staggered. Both by how quickly Maddie worked—to her inexperienced eye the painting looked almost finished—and by the incredible sensuality that leapt off the canvas. There was a languidness in the pose that suggested the aftermath of a torrid session of lovemaking. One could almost picture a soft smile of satisfaction lingering on the unseen lips of the model.

But the model was *herself*! she remembered with a gasp. And she no more knew what the aftermath of a torrid session of lovemaking was like than . . . than . . .

'You don't like it,' Maddie pronounced, pouting.

Carolyn straightened her shoulders. 'No, it's breathtaking,' she reassured. 'But . . . it isn't me.'

'Oh, it's you all right, Carolyn. The you you keep hidden from yourself, as well as everyone else. But not for much longer, I'll warrant.'

'What . . . what do you mean?'

'Come now,' came the drawled reply. 'You and I both know you're going to have an affair with Vaughan sooner or later. It's just a question of how long you'll hold out.'

CHAPTER EIGHT

CAROLYN was surprised to find herself enjoying the party that night. Maddie's prophecy of doom had haunted her for the rest of the afternoon, even though she'd pooh-poohed the idea at the time with a suitable amount of firm indifference. Maddie had simply shrugged and said, 'We'll see' with an infuriating smugness.

But by the time a few hours had passed and Maddie had funnelled several lethal-looking cocktails down Carolyn's throat, the future wasn't looking quite so worrying. Carolyn even succumbed to Maddie making up her face, though she refused to let her curl her hair.

'It's bad enough, leaving it out,' she'd stated.

And now, it was ten o'clock, the party was in full swing, and Carolyn was discoing with a tall thin chap who'd been eyeing her since he arrived. A local dentist, he was a surprisingly good dancer, and had succeeded in getting the normally inhibited Carolyn to really open up. Though perhaps her lack of reserve was due to the couple of glasses of Chardonnay that had followed the earlier cocktails rather than her partner's skill.

The music abruptly changed to an even more foot-tapping number and more people got to their feet. The room became so crowded that Carolyn and the dentist and several other couples spilled out on to the back veranda, which Maddie had thankfully cleared of all painting equipment and half-finished nudes.

'Hey, you're great!' the dancing dentist complimented when Carolyn executed a couple of the more adventurous steps she'd seen on television.

'You're not too bad yourself,' she called back over the loudly throbbing beat.

'I've never seen you at one of Maddie's parties before.'

'I've never been!'

'You married?'

'Nope.'

'Engaged?'

'Not at the moment.'

'Involved with anyone?'

Carolyn opened her mouth to answer. And froze.

Vaughan was standing in the archway leading out on to the veranda, staring at her, a tight hard look on his face. She gulped, one hand lifting to nervously push several long blonde trails of hair back from her face and shoulders, all the while hotly conscious of Vaughan's piercing brown eyes taking in everything about her, from her loosely flowing hair to her elaborately made-up face to her newly lush curves, hardly hidden in the now much tighter red crêpe sheath.

'What's up?' Her partner's head swivelled on his shoulders to encounter Vaughan's none too pleased glare. 'Oh-oh,' he muttered. 'I knew it was too good to be true. The boyfriend, I gather?'

Carolyn blinked. Then rallied. For pity's sake, what was the matter with her? Fancy letting Vaughan spoil her fun like this! But despite her self-criticism she could not seem to resume dancing in front of him.

An agitated sound escaped her lips. Perhaps it would be better if she went over and spoke to him, told him her news about moving into Julian's house. After all, it had to be done eventually. What better place than here, in a crowded room?

'He's not my boyfriend,' she informed her companion. 'Merely a business acquaintance. One I didn't expect to see here tonight. I'm sorry, but I must speak to him. Can we continue this dance later?'

'Why does something tell me that later will never come?' he said with a resigned sigh.

'Pessimist,' Carolyn laughed.

'No, a realist. Oh, well...' He was already searching the crowd for any spare females.

Carolyn kept her chin up as she walked the short distance across the veranda towards Vaughan. Contrary to Maddie's insistence that people did not come to her parties in jeans and a T-shirt, Vaughan was wearing just that. The jeans were greyish, the T-shirt white. Both clung like second skins.

Carolyn swallowed. Now she knew what her girlfriends had seen in him all those years ago. But the more her heart hammered in her chest, the more she was determined to control her unfortunate weakness for this man's body.

'Vaughan,' she said with superb coolness. 'What brings you here? Maddie said you were working tonight.'

He somehow slid his hands into the pockets of his jeans, even though Carolyn would have sworn there couldn't possibly be any room.

'I was,' he said. 'But I couldn't concentrate.'

'Can I get you a drink?' she asked, her tone perfectly civil, but icily distant.

Too bad she couldn't do much about her flushed cheeks. Though she reckoned he would put them down to dancing, not desire.

'Vaughan! You came!' Maddie materialised beside them, a tall bluish cocktail in one hand, a beer in the other. She was wearing a long black Indian caftan, which at first glance was astonishingly modest for Maddie, till one noticed the lacy side panels and lack of underwear. 'How dare you sneak in without letting me know?' she chided playfully, though with a quick frowning glance at Carolyn. When she received an apparently indifferent shrug in return, Maddie visibly relaxed.

'I knocked,' Vaughan said, his eyes never leaving Carolyn's face. 'But you didn't answer.'

'Here, have this beer. Sorry, but I can't hear anyone at the front door from the back of the house.'

'So I finally gathered,' he muttered, extracting his hands to take the beer and sip some of the froth from the top. His eyes didn't desert Carolyn's for more than a second. When he lowered the glass, a white dollop stayed on his upper lip, drawing her gaze. She found herself staring at his mouth. When the tip of his tongue flicked out and wiped the dollop slowly away, her whole stomach turned over. 'Not that anyone could hear anything much over that music,' he added drily.

Carolyn bristled. 'It's good dancing music.'

'I could see that.' His eyes dropped down the full length of her, then up again. 'Watching you dance was quite an . . . experience.'

She laughed. It provided a minimal release to the excruciating tension that was gripping her whole body. 'What a predictably male comment!'

'Oh, dear,' Maddie groaned. 'You two aren't going to fight again, are you?'

'That certainly wasn't my intention in coming here,' Vaughan snapped.

'Thank God for that. Now . . . Who was I getting this drink for? Aah, yes . . . Melissa. Don't worry, Melissa, darling,' she called back into the house. 'I haven't forgotten you! Now you be nice to Carolyn, you brute,' Maddie warned as she moved off, 'or you'll have me to answer to!'

Once she was alone with Vaughan, even the rock music couldn't prevent the harrowing effect of a strained silence between them. In the end, Carolyn could not bear Vaughan's dark, intensely provocative gaze any longer. 'What is it you keep staring at?' she challenged, pushing another wayward strand of hair back behind her ear.

'Where would you like me to start?' he asked, sounding almost angry. And definitely reproachful.

'I thought you said you didn't want a fight. If you start picking on me or my appearance again, I can assure you you'll get one.'

He made a scoffing sound. 'Well, you have to admit that it's hard to compare the prim, grey-suited virgin of a few weeks ago with the scarlet-garbed rager you've turned into tonight. Though perhaps you have a new sexual status to go with your new look.'

She sucked in a furious, shaking breath, expelling it in a rush of hot air and angry words. 'How dare you use that judgemental tone with me?' she hissed. 'You, who wouldn't know right from wrong if it bit you on the nose. You, who sleep with every woman who flutters her eyelashes at you. You, whose idea of moral restraint is to wait till a man dies before you screw his wife!'

She scraped in another ragged lungful of air. 'If you must know, my sexual status hasn't changed one iota. Though what would it matter to a man like you if I were a virgin or not?' she threw at him. 'Why the hell should you care?'

For a long long moment he said nothing, merely glared at her over his drink. Then quite abruptly, he put down the beer on a nearby shelf and reached out to take hold of her shoulders, peering down at her with steely eyes. 'Because I *do* care,' he insisted. 'Why, I've no idea, since you patently despise me. But that doesn't seem to stop my mind filling with your image every waking moment, doesn't stop my body aching to touch you, kiss you, make love to you. Goddammit, Carolyn,' he grated out, his fingers digging deep into her shoulder blades, 'I want you. And I know you want me. You damned well *told* me you do!'

She stared up at him, eyes wide, heart pounding.

Don't listen to him, her conscience screamed at her. And don't, for pity's sake, admit to another darned thing.

'How...how did you know I'd be here?' she asked shakily.

Her change of subject threw him momentarily. 'Does it matter?'

Maddie, she thought. She must have rung Vaughan while I was in the shower. God, I'll kill her!

'All that matters,' Vaughan growled impatiently, 'is that you put aside all these ridiculously old-fashioned prejudices you have against me and face facts. There's a chemistry between us, Carolyn, that won't be denied. I'm fed up with fighting it—*and you*!—for no good reason.'

Carolyn wrenched away from his hold and pulled herself up straight, anger giving her the strength to struggle against the insidious temptation he kept putting in her path.

'No good reason,' she scorned with a low, bitter laugh. 'Now isn't that just like you, Vaughan Slater. But, contrary to your free-and-easy values, I'll have you know that there would be a lot of girls—not old-fashioned ones either—who would balk at going to bed with their mother's ex-lover, no matter how much they desired him!'

His head rocked back as though she had struck him. 'My God,' he exclaimed in a husky whisper. Before she could do anything to stop him, he stepped forward and cupped her face in his hands, forcing her to look deep into his eyes.

'Carolyn,' he stated firmly, 'I did not sleep with your mother. I *never* slept with your mother. Hell...no wonder you've been upset and angry with me. I had no idea you thought...'

His expression darkened to one of black exasperation and his hands dropped from her face. 'Did Isabel claim I'd actually slept with her?' he demanded to know.

'N...no,' she stammered, trying desperately to make some sense of this most astonishing assertion. 'But...but...what about what I saw that night? You were both only half dressed. You were kissing each other...touching. You didn't even know I was there! My God, you can't expect me to believe you didn't make love!'

'But we *didn't*! I swear to you, Carolyn. I'm not lying. Bloody hell,' he groaned, and raked agitated fingers through his hair.

'You did *kiss* her,' she accused, unwilling and unable to let go the black image of this man she had built up. His being bad was her protection.

His grimace was as good as a confession in Carolyn's eyes. 'Look, you don't understand. I'd just finished my final exams that day and when I came home Isabel had... Well, she...' He broke off and shot Carolyn a frustrated look, muttering something under his breath.

His sigh, when it came, was ragged. 'I suppose I can't honestly say what might have happened if I hadn't heard the sound of a door banging.'

A door banging...

Carolyn thought of herself, fleeing from the house in great distress, letting the wire door slam behind her.

'I thought it might be you,' he elaborated. 'The idea of your catching me with your mother the way we were appalled me, but...' He broke off again, his face showing more frustration. 'Isabel swore it couldn't be you home yet from ballet, and when I looked through the house it *was* empty. But still, I...we...couldn't continue. I certainly never...'

Suddenly one of the gyrating partygoers knocked violently into Carolyn's back. Vaughan eased her away from the apologising dancer, irritation on his face. 'Look, I can't even hear myself think in here with that music, let alone all this pushing and shoving. Let's get out of here. We'll go to my place where we can at least talk in peace.'

His place? He wanted her to go to his place, where they'd be alone together?

Why not? the voice of temptation silkily inserted. He's just told you he wasn't your mother's lover. Wasn't that the main impediment against your risking being alone in his company?

Well, yes...

And no...

'What about the board money?' she blurted out.

'The board money?' He simply stared at her in blank confusion. 'What in heaven's name are you talking about?'

'You didn't pay,' she went on in a rush, her heart pounding madly. 'Those last few months you stayed at our place. You didn't pay. *Why* didn't you pay?'

Vaughan's sigh was an angry one. 'I *did* pay.' He shook his head slowly from side to side. 'Oh, Carolyn, Carolyn... just how low an opinion of me do you have? Look, the situation was that my father died that year and all of a sudden there wasn't any money to supplement my government student subsidy, which hardly covered my books and general living expenses. I told Isabel I could no longer afford the board we'd agreed on and that I would have to move to cheaper digs. She insisted that I stay and just pay what I could. I got some local work mowing lawns and gardening, and handed over whatever I earned in cash. I did *not* pay for my board with the sort of services you've obviously been envisaging,' he finished with a hefty dose of bitter reproach.

Carolyn didn't know whether to feel ashamed, or ecstatic. All she knew was that a great weight had been lifted from her heart.

'Do I rate an apology at last?' he ground out.

'Well I . . . I . . .'

'It's gratifying to see that I rattle you almost as much as you rattle me. Come, Carolyn,' he growled, taking her wrist in an iron grip, 'we've tortured each other long enough. It's time to bring this fiasco to its natural conclusion.'

Giving her body an all encompassing and highly stirring look, he started dragging her dazed self through the dancing drinking laughing throng, till a tall black figure moved abruptly into their path.

'And where do you think you're taking Carolyn?' Maddie demanded with arched eyebrows.

'Home,' came Vaughan's brusk reply.

'Your home or her home?'

'*Mine*,' he snapped. 'Any objections?'

Maddie threw Carolyn a sharp look, taking in her high colour and the rapid rise and fall of her breasts. A wry smile tugged at her scarlet-glossed mouth. 'Not if the lady hasn't——'

'She hasn't,' Vaughan bit out.

'She has a tongue of her own, doesn't she? Well, Carolyn? Do you want to go with this . . . neanderthal?'

Carolyn was taken aback by the slightly anxious light in her friend's eyes. How odd, she thought breathlessly. Hadn't this been Maddie's intention in getting Vaughan to come? Hadn't she been playing matchmaker behind her back? Why should she worry now if Vaughan wanted to take her off and make mad, passionate love to her?

Carolyn's mind raced back over her last words. Make mad, passionate love ...

A compulsive combination of excitement and anticipation charged through her body, and she knew that nothing and no one could stop her from going with Vaughan at that moment.

'Yes,' she choked out. 'I do.'

If anything, Maddie's anxiety increased, confusing Carolyn all the more. But then the other woman shrugged, as though resigned to the inevitable. 'So be it,' she nodded. 'But before you go...'

Sweeping over to her built-in black bar, she returned with a bottle of champagne, pressing the chilled bottle into Carolyn's free hand. 'Nothing like champagne to make a party swing along,' she laughed. 'Even if it *is* a private one.' Leaning close, she whispered, 'Be careful, sweetie. Just an affair, remember? Don't fall in love with him.'

Carolyn had no time to comment before Vaughan swept her away and out into the night.

CHAPTER NINE

MADDIE had been overly critical of Vaughan's home, Carolyn thought dazedly when the maroon MG screeched into the driveway of a beautiful old wooden house with high-pitched ceilings, huge verandas all around and the most entrancing stained-glass windows. Admittedly, the cream paintwork needed redoing, and the lawns and gardens could have done with some attention. But the house had true charm and grandeur, perched as it was on the highest point of a cliff overlooking the Pacific Ocean and the cutest little beach Carolyn had ever seen.

Thoughts of houses, however, were dashed from Carolyn's mind when Vaughan strode round to wrench open the passenger door, giving her a searing glance before extending a large, very male hand. She swallowed, her much smaller softer fingers shaking as she placed them within his strong, aggressive grip.

Not a word had passed between them on the short trip over, the silence emphasising the mad pounding of her heart. It leapt when she felt his fingers close tightly around her hand, a spurt of adrenalin charging through her body.

Did she really know what she was doing? Or didn't she care any more? She certainly didn't seem to. Somehow, Vaughan's revealing he had not been her mother's lover had let go the floodgates of her passion, so long dammed back by her conscience.

She raised fluttering lashes to his beautiful yet ruthlessly determined eyes, frowning as Maddie's warning flashed back into her mind.

Will I fall in love with him if I do this? she wondered in a panic. I don't want to. I *mustn't*! Just because he never made love to my mother doesn't wipe out the fact that she loved him and had a nervous breakdown over him. There's no permanent place in my life for this man.

'Don't look so worried,' he muttered. 'I don't bite. We-ll...' His slow smile was incredibly sexy. 'Only gently, and only where required.'

He laughed at her furious blush, then hauled her out of the car, gathering her to him in a breathlessly close embrace. 'God, I want you,' he rasped, and she actually felt him shudder. 'To think that the only thing standing between us all these weeks was a stupid misunderstanding...'

Groaning, he pulled her even closer, holding the back of her head while he covered her mouth with a hungry kiss, sending his tongue between her gasping lips in a passionate sortie with her own. It was ages before he let her come up for air. 'Much as I'd like to continue,' he sighed raggedly, 'I think I should go for a short swim first. I've been working all day. Well...*trying* to work,' he amended with a low sensual chuckle. 'I want to feel cool and clean and in much better control when I finally make love to you, my darling. This is a moment for perfection, not some hurried tumble on the grass.'

Carolyn's mind whirled with his evocative words. And then with another of his kisses. A slower one this time, infinitely slower, yet deeper and more intimate and excruciatingly stirring. 'Tell me you'll deny me nothing,' he urged fiercely. 'Tell me you'll let me do all the things I've been wanting to do to you.'

Stunned by the alarming content and sheer intensity of his words, she could do nothing but blink glazed eyes at him.

'I've shocked you,' he muttered, regret in his voice. And bent to give her a softer, gentler kiss. 'Sorry... I keep forgetting how innocent you are...how sweetly delightfully irritatingly innocent.' His smile was an odd mixture of apology and irony. 'I'll go more slowly from now on. You don't have to be frightened. I won't hurt you. I promise... Come... Let's put this champagne on ice and go for that swim together.'

Of course he would hurt her, Carolyn agonised as he led her up the old stone steps. If not physically, then certainly emotionally. But that was the price she would have to pay for this one insane, glorious night with him.

The inside of the house proved to be as untidy as Maddie had predicted. Not that Carolyn gave a hoot about a little mess at that moment. She wouldn't have cared if Vaughan had thrown her down in a pigsty and taken her in the mud, so besotted was she by the feelings his kisses had evoked in her. Her heart was beating like a thousand butterflies' wings. Her whole body felt like it was on a perpetual high, every nerve-ending seemingly electrified.

Vaughan put the bottle of champagne in the fridge in the colonial-style kitchen, then led her back through the littered living-room down the airy hallway and into a relatively tidy bedroom. He left her standing beside the huge brass bed—which was, surprisingly, made—and walked over to a solid mahogany chest of drawers. Without hesitation, he stripped off his T-shirt and jeans and threw them over a chair, standing in front of her quite unconsciously in brief navy underpants while he fished out his white swimming trunks from a drawer. Then without blinking an eyelid, but thankfully with his back turned towards her, the underpants went the same way as the jeans, though quickly replaced by the minute Lycra costume.

When he turned Carolyn tried not to stare. For his body was hardly in repose, and the small costume was proving inadequate.

'Yes,' he stated drily. 'A cooling swim is definitely in order. Now...what can I get for you to wear? Or do you fancy a bit of skinny-dipping?'

Carolyn's heart leapt. It was, after all, only elevenish on a Saturday night. One could hardly guarantee the beach would be deserted. Immediately, she thought of the new black underwear she was wearing. Modest, she supposed, by modern bikini standards. Without waiting for Vaughan to offer to undress her—or her courage to fail her—Carolyn crossed her arms and whipped the red crêpe dress over her head, tossing it on to the bed. Not having worn stockings, all she had to do was kick off her black high heels and she was as ready as she'd ever be for a moonlight dip.

'Hell's bells!' Vaughan exclaimed, looking her up and down. 'Is that supposed to cool my ardour?'

Quite unbidden, a naughty little smile pulled at her lips. 'I hope not.'

A wry grin split his face. 'You do realise, my sweet, that you're seriously testing my reputation as a lover.'

'Am I?' she husked, feeling more wickedly sensual than she ever had in her life.

There was a steep path, leading from the cliff down to the cove. Once down on the moonlit sand, Carolyn was to discover that next to the tiny beach, near the rocks, was a man-made pool, quite large and full of sea-water. It looked like a peaceful lagoon down the end near the beach, but there was plenty of wild water down the other where waves kept crashing over the cement wall, sending spray high into the air. A couple of young lads were standing on top of the wall in the moonlight, bravely or foolishly enjoying the thrills of the waves and spray hitting them.

As Carolyn watched, both dived back into the pool in the face of an unexpectedly big wave, then immediately climbed out and waited for another.

'Isn't that dangerous?' she asked Vaughan, and shivered.

'A little. But life's full of dangers. And risks. Sometimes, it's better to face them head on than to always take the safer, more timid approach. Such experiences give one courage, and spirit.'

A tremor coursed through Carolyn with Vaughan's remark. For that was what she was doing tonight. Taking a risk...a *huge* risk. For Vaughan was like that rogue wave, higher and stronger and more dangerous than the rest. He engulfed women with his powerful sex appeal, picked them up and

carried them along for a while on his crest of
passion before dumping them down and with-
drawing, abandoning them like so much flotsam
on the empty shore of shattered souls.

Her thudding heart almost jumped out of her
chest when he suddenly snaked a possessive hand
around her bare waist, turning her and pulling her
hard against him. His other hand slid up beneath
her hair where he cupped the back of her neck and
held her face captive for a succession of brief,
hungry kisses.

'God, Carolyn,' he groaned. 'I can't stand much
more of this! This will have to be the quickest swim
on record.' And taking her by the hand, he dragged
her with him into the moonlit sea.

Less than five minutes later Carolyn was back in
Vaughan's bedroom, sitting on the edge of his huge
bed. Vaughan was kneeling up behind her and
trying to rub her hair dry with a towel.

'I should have put it up,' she moaned.

'It's my fault,' he soothed, and, pushing the
damp mass to one side, pressed hot lips against the
back of her neck. 'We'll have you warmed up soon
enough,' he promised on a husky whisper.

Carolyn began to shiver uncontrollably.

Quite abruptly, Vaughan abandoned her and slid
off the bed. 'Come on,' he advised in a firm voice.
'Take those wet undies off and get into bed while
I go rustle up that champagne Maddie gave us.
Nothing like a glass of bubbly to warm a chilled
bloodstream. *Yours*, not mine,' he added drily as
he strode from the room.

By the time he returned with the opened bottle
of champagne and two crystal fluted glasses,

Carolyn had hastily dried her hair some more, stripped off and dived under the covers. Vaughan stopped in the doorway and stared at her, perched up against a myriad pillows, the top sheet firmly clutched up over her naked breasts.

He frowned at the obvious fear in her face before letting his gaze linger on the way her nearly dry honey-blonde hair had fluffed out in erotic disarray over her bare shoulders. With a frustrated sigh he moved over to place the bottle and glasses on the bedside table, then sat down on the bed, where with authoritative, economical movements he poured the wine, filling one glass to the brim, the other only halfway.

Carolyn guessed which one would be hers before he handed it over. She took the full glass with shaking fingers and tried to stop staring at Vaughan's near-naked body. But the intimacy of the bedroom as well as the imminence of what they were about to do kept producing wildly opposite responses within her. She felt aroused and afraid at the same time. One part of her ached for him to start making love to her. The other was terrified of the outcome, both physically and emotionally.

'Let's make a toast,' he suggested, and clicked her glass with his. 'To...love?'

Her heart turned over and her gaze dropped from his. Why on earth did he choose such a toast? Surely he wasn't expecting her to say she *loved* him, was he?

And then it came to her.

Perhaps this was what he always did with women: made such ambivalent remarks, unconsciously giving his prospective bed partners reason to believe he loved them without his actually saying so. Perhaps he needed a temporary emotional closeness to enjoy sex, but, once his physical desires were sated, any talk of love disappeared. Which, of course, could very well leave a confused woman with a broken heart—like her mother. Carolyn didn't think he meant to hurt women. He just did.

Slowly her eyes rose, a somewhat bleak resolve in her heart. She would play along with him, this one time, for this one night. But in the morning...

Lifting the glass, she forced a smile to her lips. 'To love,' she said, then moved the quivering glass toward her lips, thinking to herself that she had never needed a drink more in her life.

But her hand was shaking so much she spilt some, a small stream of the sparkling liquid missing her mouth, cascading from the rim of the glass off her chin and down on to her chest.

Carolyn was mortified, an embarrassed heat flooding her neck and face. 'Oh, God... I'm so stupid, I...' She went to mop up the disaster with the sheet she had clutched in her other hand, but only succeeded in spilling some more champagne. The chilled liquid splashed down on to her heated skin and began to trickle down the valley between her breasts. She squealed and dropped the sheet altogether, totally baring herself to Vaughan's eyes.

Smoothly and without any fuss he swept the glass from her hand, depositing it with his own back on the bedside table before returning to grip both her trembling hands in his and push her gently but firmly back into the pillows.

'Stop getting yourself all in a dither,' he growled softly, and kissed her. 'I'll have you nice and dry in no time...' And without releasing her hands he actually bent his mouth to where the champagne had first landed, and began licking the wet skin.

Carolyn's startled lips fell open, her breathing suspended while she watched him move down over her body, her eyes widening as she felt her body responding to the feel of his lips and tongue on her flesh. Her breasts swelled with visible arousal, both nipples peaking, hard and almost painful. She tried to free her hands from his—to do she knew not what—but he held her fast, entwining her fingers with his, imprisoning her hands on each side of her while he continued to enslave her body with his erotic ministrations.

Once the spilled champagne was dealt with, he moved on to her breasts, moistening the taut peaks with his tongue before drawing first one, then the other, into the hot cavern of his mouth. Carolyn was staggered by the shafts of sensation that shot through her every time he did this, for her response wasn't anywhere near her breasts. It was deep in her stomach, contracting sharply before burning a searing path down between her thighs. Soon, her limbs grew restless with an alien agitation. She wanted to move her legs, her hips, her back. She wanted to arch up into his body, to press into him, to have his hard hot flesh closer and closer to hers.

Finally, she moaned, partly to drag in some more air, but mainly as an expression of the intense frustration coursing through her. She wanted Vaughan physically. But she wanted his love more; wanted him to hold her close and tell her he loved her as much as she loved him.

A tortured groan was torn from her lips in denial of what she'd just conceded. I can't have fallen in love with him, she tried telling herself. I *can't!*

But of course she had. Deeply. Despairingly.

Oh, God ... How could she have been so stupid?

Once again, she tried to tear away from his grasp, only to have his eyes snap up and lance her with an impassioned glare. 'Stop it!' he growled, taking her hands and stretching them up over her head, curling her fingers round one of the brass railings of the bed-head. 'This is what you want,' he reproached thickly. 'What you need. What we *both* need. There's no going back now, Carolyn. No stopping. No running away. I mean to make you mine, every glorious inch of you. So stop fighting me, my love. It's useless, anyway. You're as much my slave as I am yours.'

And with a raw naked groan he bent his mouth—*and* his hands—to her body once more.

Carolyn bit her bottom lip against the tumultuous pleasure he immediately evoked, her knuckles whitening around the railing as she felt him gradually work his way back down her body. Surely he didn't mean to... to...

When he passed her navel, every internal muscle she owned contracted and held tightly. Her lips parted, as though ready for protest. But no protest came from her lips when he finally reached his destination. No protest at all. Only a shuddering sigh of sheer ecstasy. 'Oh, yes,' she moaned. 'Yes...'

Carolyn would have willingly endured this exquisite torture forever, if his knowingly expert fingers hadn't joined in as well. They started a far more intimate exploration of her flesh and

gradually, things started changing. While still incredibly exciting, each bold foray into her body
seemed to twist her insides tighter and tighter, giving
her earlier blissful pleasure a decided edge.

'Vaughan!' she cried out at last.

He stopped what he was doing and loomed over
her, his face strained, his own breathing ragged.
'Carolyn,' he said with a shudder. 'Sorry, but
there's something I must do at this point... I won't
be long, my love...'

He smiled softly down at her, moving her unbearably with his thought and consideration. He
might not love her, but at least he did care.

He wasn't long. Only a few brief seconds, and
then he was back, his body splendidly naked and
still devastatingly aroused. He lay down beside her
and began to stroke her, bringing her once more to
gasping point before slowly and with infinite
gentleness fusing his desire with hers, groaning
when her superbly prepared flesh accepted his with
ease and eagerness.

Carolyn couldn't contain her own cry of astonishment. For there'd been no pain. Not even discomfort. Only the sweetest of pleasures as
Vaughan's body blended totally with hers. Emotion
moved through her like a rippling tide, flooding
her heart as well as her mind and body, uplifting
her soul with a sense of relief and wonder. How
could she have ever thought what she felt for this
man was 'just sex'?

Her arms swept around his back and she clasped
him to her heart with the tightness of love. 'Oh,
Vaughan,' she cried softly, and gulped down the
lump in her throat. For she wanted to laugh and

weep at the same time; wanted to move against his hardness, yet was also compelled to stay still, to savour the overwhelming feeling of perfect unity.

'Yes,' Vaughan said thickly. 'I feel it too. And I don't want it ever to end.' Levering himself up on his elbows he began to kiss her. On her breasts, her shoulders, her neck, her mouth. Yet all the while he was kissing her, he kept the lower half of his body perfectly still.

But very quickly Carolyn didn't want him to be still and when he kissed her again on the mouth, she clasped him closer, her nails raking his back, her hips lifting to take his flesh even further into hers. He groaned and drove his tongue deeply into her mouth, moving it back and forth in a frantic hungry rhythm as though trying to satisfy his passion that way. But in the end the rest of his body would not be denied and it started moving likewise.

Carolyn was soon beside herself, soaring on a plateau of physical passion and pleasure that carried no inhibition, no shyness. She wrapped her legs higher and harder around him, bursting from his mouth as urgent moans of desire and need punched from her lungs. Vaughan immediately picked up rhythm, holding her tightly beneath him, surging powerfully into her eager, straining body.

For a split second Carolyn felt a thrilling moment of peaking, of being suspended. And then she was spun into a wild avalanche of sensation that shattered her completely, the experience impossible to fully capture in words or even memory. Its sharpness caught at her breath, then forced sounds from her lips, soft sensual cries somewhere between sighs and moans. Her head tipped back, her lips panting apart, her back bending like a bow from the bed as she felt her flesh convulsing around Vaughan's, felt her woman's pull on his body, urging him to a mutual release.

When it came Carolyn was stunned, thinking the pleasure she'd just experienced was impossible to surpass. But nothing could eclipse the emotional and physical satisfaction of holding Vaughan and feeling him climax deep within her. She thrilled to his raw groans of pleasure, to his shuddering muscles, to the way he finally sank down on top of her and buried his gasping mouth in her hair.

They sighed together, content and exhausted. And didn't move for ages.

'I don't think I'll ever stir again,' she said dreamily when Vaughan rejoined her after a brief trip to the bathroom. Trailing a limp hand over his muscular chest, she smiled at him with heavy-lidded eyes.

He lifted her hand to his mouth and kissed each fingertip in turn. 'You *will* stir again. I mean to stir you on and off for the rest of the night... But a small sleep first might be in order...'

When the dawn came, Carolyn conceded she hadn't slept much, though Vaughan had at long last succumbed to exhaustion and was fast asleep beside her. She sighed as she glanced over at him and thought of how, during those long waking hours, he'd brought her over and over to that exquisite release, each time taking her a little further into the world of sensual pleasure. She learnt what it was to make love to a man, to pleasure him as much as he pleasured her, to take and give with no holding back, no shame. Only love.

Her heart squeezed tight at this thought. For of course, it hadn't been real love on Vaughan's part. Just sex. Or lust. Or animal need. Or whatever men like him deigned to call it. One woman was pretty well as good as another, she imagined with a bleak understanding. The only reason he'd become temporarily besotted with her was because she'd resisted him for so long. Or maybe because she was much more inexperienced than his usual conquest. Perhaps he'd seen her innocence as an irresistible challenge.

Well . . . her innocence had been totally shattered last night. She had surrendered to him as completely as a woman could to a man. Physically *and* emotionally. How she managed to last the whole night without saying aloud how much she loved him was a miracle. But it was to be thanked she hadn't. Such an admission would have rendered futile what she was about to do.

A sudden weakness clutched at her heart, tempting her to procrastinate, but she swiftly swept it aside. The sooner this was done, the better!

Mustering all her courage, she sat up and swung her legs less than quietly over the side of the bed. As was her intention, Vaughan stirred.

'Where are you off to?' he asked sleepily.

'To the bathroom,' came her curt reply. 'Then after I'm dressed I'd appreciate it if you could please drive me back to Maddie's.'

'*What*?' His hand gripped her shoulder and he twisted her round to face him. 'But *why*? Maddie will be out for the count for most of the day. I thought we'd spend the rest of the weekend together. I thought... Hell, what's got into you this morning? You *enjoyed* last night, didn't you?'

Carolyn swallowed. Dear heaven, but this was the hardest thing she had ever done in her life. But she had to. She just had to! How could she possibly introduce Vaughan to her mother as her lover, however temporary? Impossible. It was too cruel. She had to cut dead this relationship once and for all!

'Of course I enjoyed it,' she said, distress giving her words a bitter edge. 'Too much.' She yanked out of his hold and stood up, dragging a covering sheet with her. Unfortunately, this particular sheet was the only thing between Vaughan and total nudity, which was hardly what Carolyn needed to confront at that moment.

'Too much?' he repeated, a disbelieving note in his voice. 'How can you like sex too much?'

His use of the word 'sex' instead of 'making love' struck her raw emotions like the flick of a bull-whip, and she shuddered. But at least it reinforced Vaughan's view of what they'd done together. And gave her the strength to continue.

'I would imagine,' she began, keeping her eyes and voice as steady as possible, 'that it would be much easier to walk away from a one-night stand if one hadn't enjoyed it quite so much.'

His frown was immediate and dark. 'A one-night stand?' His eyes were like hot brown coals, searing into her, burning her. 'Is that how you think of last night?'

'What else?' she tossed off, her heart breaking.

'*What else*?' He stared at her for a few seconds then gave a harsh bark of laughter. 'I take it, then,' he ground out sarcastically, 'that I'm not to be privileged with a repeat performance tonight, or any other night?'

'You take it correctly. Goodness, Vaughan, why all the hearts and flowers? You and I both know that the only thing between us was a sexual attraction.'

'*Was*?' He lifted an incredulous eyebrow.

Her shrug was superbly indifferent. 'Well, I think we went a long way to dampening the fires last night, don't you? I'm quite exhausted.'

'Now let me get this straight...' He climbed off the bed to stand with legs apart and hands on hips. Dressed, it would have been an angry, aggressive stance. Naked, it was both threatening and disturbing. 'You want me to believe that a girl who scorns casual sex, who hauled me over the coals for using women's bodies without a scrap of feeling, that this same girl has just surrendered her innocence without being in love? You were merely scratching an itch, so to speak?'

Carolyn cringed at these last words.

'Answer me, damn you!' he roared, grabbing her and shaking her violently.

'Yes,' she croaked.

'Liar!' He released her with a savage twist, his face full of frustration. 'Hell, don't take me for a fool, Carolyn. I know you now. And I don't mean just in the Biblical sense. I know what makes you tick, what values have shaped your life, what sort of person you are. You have deep, deep feelings. And standards. You didn't keep your virginity all these years to throw it away lightly. You love me, woman. Why won't you admit it? What's the real reason behind this trumped-up garbage? Is this still because of your stupid damned mother?'

'You're the one who's being stupid,' she retorted angrily. 'A virgin can lust as much as the next person, believe me. Maybe more, even, since virginity is a totally unnatural state for a normal healthy twenty-four-year-old woman. If you want your ego stroked, Vaughan, then let me tell you that you're one hell of a sexy guy. A veritable lady-killer! Even Maddie knew it was just a matter of time before I ended up in your bed. I'm sure that's why she rang you yesterday and told you where I'd be. She probably thought the sooner I got it over with, the better.'

'God, you make me sound like a case of the chicken pox!' he snapped. 'And for your information, Maddie *didn't* ring me.'

Carolyn was floored by this news. 'She *didn't*? But . . . but last night you said . . . I mean . . .'

'I knew you'd stay for the party.'

She simply looked blank.

He made a frustrated sound. 'I went round to Maddie's earlier in the afternoon. She didn't answer the front door, so I . . . Well, I . . .' Suddenly, he looked uncomfortable.

Understanding dawned on Carolyn.

'So you came round the back and saw Maddie painting me through the window,' she finished bitterly. 'You stood there and watched, didn't you? Seeing me naked turned you on, didn't it? That's why you came to the party. Simply and solely to scratch *your* itch!' She glowered at him. 'And you dare to demand that I sanctify my one and only sexual transgression with deeper feelings. *You*, who have never been in love in his life. *You*, whose only feelings for a woman are strictly below the waist!'

She scooped in a shuddering breath and went on, her tirade fuelled by fury at fate for letting her fall in love with such a man. 'Believe me when I say I not only don't love you, Vaughan Slater, I despise you, almost as much as I despise myself for having let you touch me at all.'

He stared at her for a long long moment, a stony mask dropping over his face. It rather shocked her, for she was used to being able to read his emotions through his expressive eyes. But his eyes were suddenly cold. Cold and hard. Totally without feeling. Frightened, she lifted a defensive hand to her throat and took a backward step, almost tripping over the sheet.

'Is that so?' he said in a voice like ice. 'Too bad. I really was hoping for an encore. But you're quite right, Carolyn. That's exactly what happened. I saw you lying there without a stitch of clothing on and I wanted you. I left but I couldn't get the sight of your undeniably desirable and nymph-like body out of my mind. In the end, I decided I had to have you, no matter what. So, yes...I came to that party, determined to get you into my bed, determined to do whatever it took to make you succumb to all those crude desires you once confessed to.'

His smile was chilling. 'And I succeeded, didn't I?'

Suddenly, his jaw clenched tightly. 'Now get your clothes on and get the hell out of my life.'

All the blood drained from Carolyn's face. She thought of that moment—eons ago, it seemed—

when Vaughan had looked at her and vowed, 'One day, Carolyn. One day...'

Well, the day had been yesterday.

The sound of a telephone ringing cut across the strained silence. Vaughan gave her one last cold, hard look, and strode from the room.

Carolyn stared after his retreating figure, her mind and heart still reeling. She tried telling herself that it was all for the best, but nothing could soften the distress she felt at thinking that all the while she'd been making love to Vaughan, he'd been smugly triumphant over her surrender. It made her feel used and despoiled and more than a little sick.

But finally, acceptance of the awful truth galvanised her into action. She dressed swiftly then fled the bedroom, unfortunately having to pass through the living-room on the way to the front door. A still naked Vaughan was standing there, with the receiver at his ear, looking and sounding so ghastly that Carolyn ground to a startled halt.

'Oh, no,' he groaned. 'Oh, Jesse... Why now, when everything was coming right for her... Poor Mum... Yes... I'll come at once... No... Don't worry... I'll take care of it... See you tonight... Bye...'

Carolyn guessed immediately what had happened. Vaughan's mother had died.

His shoulders slumped as he dropped the receiver into its cradle and Carolyn instinctively ached to go to him. There was no reasoning at times like this. All she wanted was to soothe and comfort the man she loved in this, his hour of need.

She walked slowly forward and laid a tentative hand on his shoulder. 'Vaughan... is there... anything I can do?'

She rocked backwards when he turned to look at her. Never had she seen such pain. 'Yes... Just get out. Get out and leave me alone.'

CHAPTER TEN

'AND SO you left,' Maddie sighed.

'Yes.' Carolyn burst into tears again.

Maddie pushed the box of tissues in front of her. They were already half gone.

'I...I didn't want to,' Carolyn sobbed. 'But when I tried to say something else he...he gave me such a terrible look that I...I just ran.'

'All the way to Thirroul?'

'No...Vaughan came after me in his car.'

'He *did*?'

Carolyn wiped her nose. 'He made me get in, then drove me here in the most awful silence. It was horrible.'

Maddie sighed again. 'I can imagine. Are you sure about his mother dying, though? I mean...you could be wrong, couldn't you?'

She shook her head. 'I don't think so.'

'Neither do I, actually.'

'I...I never thought of Vaughan as having a family,' Carolyn said brokenly. 'I...I guess I don't really know him at all, despite everything.'

'Carolyn,' Maddie said firmly, 'I think it's time you told me exactly what's been going on with you and Vaughan. And no, I don't mean about last night. It's perfectly clear what happened there. He made beautiful love to you and you're mad about him. What I want to know is *why* you're so torn up about it, and why in heaven's name you can't keep sleeping with him, even if he doesn't love you or want to marry you? Which I could have predicted, I might add. Some men are the marrying kind. Some aren't. But back to the point! You must tell me the whole grisly tale and we'll see what solution we can come up with.'

Maddie couldn't come up with any solution. Once she learnt Vaughan had almost become Carolyn's mother's lover, and that the poor woman had had a nervous breakdown over him, she gave up.

'What a bummer,' she said with descriptive sympathy.

'Yes,' Carolyn agreed despairingly.

'We'll have to keep Vaughan away from your mum, won't we?'

'Yes.'

'She really went to pieces over him, didn't she? I mean, how many women would start hallucinating that they'd been to bed with a guy if they hadn't? I know I certainly couldn't. I need the real thing. Still... I guess it takes all types. Your mother must be one of those fragile, vulnerable ladies who fall apart easily.'

Carolyn frowned. 'Well, no, actually... Before the day she broke down, Mum had always been a very strong lady.'

'Really?'

'Yes...' An unease settled around Carolyn's heart as a ghastly thought filtered into her brain. Could Vaughan have lied to her about not having made love to her mother? Lied in order to get the daughter into his bed as well? He'd said he'd come to the party last night, prepared to do anything to have her.

'Good grief, Carolyn, what *are* you thinking? You've gone as white as a sheet.'

Carolyn's wide eyes snapped up. 'Maddie...'

'Yes?'

'Is...is Vaughan a *wicked* man, do you think?'

Maddie was taken aback. 'Vaughan? Wicked?' She gave the matter some thought. 'Wicked is a rather ambiguous word. Do you mean evil, or just plain naughty?'

'I think I mean...evil.'

'No! Of course not! Definitely not!'

'I hope you're right,' she groaned. 'Because if you're not, then I don't know what's to become of me.'

'I'll tell you what's to become of you,' Maddie said firmly. 'Nothing bad. You're going to go on with your life, without self-pity and useless recriminations. You're going to put last night in the "valued experiences" compartment of your mind and next time you're going to fall in love with a much more suitable candidate. Now! I'll get you some healthy muesli for breakfast, and while you eat it we'll start making plans to move you down here to Wollongong.'

Carolyn gasped.

'What's wrong *now*?' Maddie asked somewhat impatiently.

'I...I never got round to telling Vaughan about that. He...I mean we—er...'

'You don't have to explain,' Maddie sighed expressively. 'I get the picture, believe me. Look, don't worry your pretty little head about a thing.

I'll tell Vaughan myself and get the keys and anything else you need. You don't have to see him again. Wollongong's a big town. And I'll invent a false name for him when your mother gets back in three weeks' time. If your mother still wants to meet him we'll say he's interstate or overseas or something. Let's just hope Julian doesn't blab his real name in the meantime. What story are you going to tell your stepfather, by the way?'

Carolyn exhaled wearily. 'God only knows.'

'I'll think of something,' Maddie offered, and patted her friend's hand.

The following days were very busy for Carolyn, what with cleaning the flat and packing and driving up and down with loads of knick-knacks and clothes, not to mention doing the thousand and one other clerical jobs associated with a major move. There were banks and insurance companies to be notified, mail to be redirected. All sorts of time-consuming tasks.

But she was grateful to be busy. It kept her mind occupied and her body tired. Each night she stayed up late till she flopped into bed, exhausted. Thoughts of Vaughan were never given much opportunity to linger. Only once did she allow herself the luxury of tears over him, and they had been more sympathy than bitterness or self-pity. For his mother *had* died, so Maddie found out. Not that she'd been able to elicit any details on the subject. Grief, Maddie said, had made Vaughan even more taciturn than usual.

So Carolyn had cried for him, knowing that everyone, even a heartless womaniser, felt the death of a mother very deeply. If she lost her own mother suddenly like that, she would be utterly devastated.

But her own mother, thank the lord, was happy and healthy. And honeymooning on the Riviera. Carolyn had been greatly relieved to receive more trouble-free postcards in which her mother made no mention of Vaughan. The only man who figured in her bright and breezy and surprisingly confident correspondence was her husband. As for Julian, he was clearly more in love with his Isabel than ever, which made Carolyn feel alternately thrilled then worried. How would he react if she was forced to reveal that his new bride had once literally gone crazy over his handsome and very sexy architect? She shuddered to think.

On the Thursday, a week before their return, all the furniture arrived at the new house as per schedule. The next day, Carolyn vacated the flat in Ashfield, her last jobs being to have the electricity and telephone disconnected. She had already disposed of all her mother's redundant furniture by advertisement in the local newspaper—her own untrustworthy Datsun had gone the same way—and had spent the last couple of nights making do with the bare essentials, sleeping on an old air-bed and eating off one set of crockery and cutlery, her only furniture a portable television set and a folding chair.

By the time Carolyn bundled herself and her last load into Julian's BMW for the final trip down to Wollongong, all her bridges had been burnt behind her. She felt quite excited about the move, despite everything. Who wouldn't be looking forward to exchanging a poky flat for such a beautiful and special home?

The ever-efficient Maddie, who'd been virtually given a blank cheque by Julian, had already stocked the new house with goods and appliances to match the décor, including linen and other items. So all Carolyn really needed to do to successfully move in was to go food shopping. Which she decided to do in Wollongong, otherwise all her freezer items would melt.

It didn't even cross her mind that she might run into Vaughan. Hadn't Maddie said Wollongong was a big town? Well, not big enough, apparently.

Carolyn was walking into an arcade, looking for the butcher's shop that the cashier in the supermarket said was there, when she spotted Vaughan sitting in the corner of a glass-walled coffee shop, looking like a well-groomed executive in a dark blue business suit and dazzling white shirt.

Her heart stopped, as well as her feet. For he wasn't alone. Anthea Maxwell was sitting opposite him. Even as Carolyn watched, the woman's hand reached out intimately to cover his on the table. She leant closer to whisper something. Vaughan nodded, then looked up with an appreciative smile on his beautiful mouth.

Carolyn's heart twisted. And to think she had allowed herself that one moment of pity for him. He didn't need pity. Or anything else from her.

Vaughan must have sensed her bitter glare for his head turned, and their eyes met. His smile faded.

Anthea Maxwell's head turned as well to see what Vaughan was looking at. Carolyn only saw the beginning of the woman's smugly superior smile. She whirled round and hurried away without buying any meat.

It didn't matter. She couldn't eat that evening anyway. She just sat on the main balcony, sipping some straight Scotch she'd found in the fully stocked bar and staring blankly at the breathtaking view of the ocean in the distance. Several large container ships dotted the horizon, perhaps making for or coming from the Port Kembla steel-works.

When she tired of watching their slow but inexorable progress—or maybe when the Scotch ran out—Carolyn went inside, showered her tipsy self, dragged on the blue silky nightie her mother had given her for Christmas, then lay down on one of the apricot leather sofas to watch TV.

A game show came on and, even though she normally liked playing along with the contestants, her distracted and unhappy mind constantly wandered from the screen. What was Vaughan doing tonight? Was he still with that horrid woman? Was he making love to her right at this moment?

The telephone interrupted her wretched thoughts, and even though she didn't want to answer, politeness insisted. It would be Maddie. The kind yet rather daunting Maddie. For she was the only person who knew the recently connected number. Levering herself up on to slightly unsteady feet, Carolyn meandered over to sink gratefully down on the chair next to the telephone. Her uncoordinated actions made her realise that drinking whisky on an empty stomach was a swift way to intoxication.

Licking dry lips, she gripped the receiver tightly and did her best to answer with a together voice. 'Hello, Maddie. What's up?'

'It's not Maddie,' Vaughan's distinctively male voice replied. 'And the only thing that's up in my life at the moment is my blood pressure.'

It took Carolyn a few seconds to get a grip on herself. And her instantaneous resentment. Who did he think he was, ringing her up and saying things like that?

But a treacherous little voice piped in, telling her he was clearly not with Anthea Maxwell. She gave a silent groan. Why, oh, why couldn't she stop her heart from leaping joyfully at that knowledge?

'Is there some purpose to this call, Vaughan?' she asked sharply, angry with herself for her weakness in still letting this man affect her.

'I want to come over and talk to you.'

Carolyn was grateful he couldn't see her shudder. 'Certainly not! If you remember rightly, you said you didn't want to see me ever again.'

A frustrated sound punched down the line. 'I've changed my mind about that.'

'Oh? And what made you change it? Wouldn't dear old Anthea come across tonight after all?'

His sigh was heavy. 'Don't be like that, Carolyn,' he said in a voice that caught at her heartstrings. 'It isn't you. Look...I'm sorry for saying that. I'm sorry for saying a lot of things. I'm coming over. I really need to talk to you.'

She could hardly believe the gall of the man. Did he honestly think she would meekly let him in?

Her laughter was bitter and cold. 'Talk, Vaughan? Since when did you want to just *talk* to a woman. Still... far be it from me to be a cynic, but if you really want to talk to me, then do so. Right now. On this telephone!'

'Goddamn it, but you're a difficult woman!' He heaved a loud, shuddering sigh. 'All right... So I don't want to just talk. I want to take you to bed too. I admit it. But it's not just sex I want, Carolyn,' he went on in a voice vibrating with the most seductive passion. 'I want *you*. Not Anthea Maxwell. Not any other woman. Only you...'

Carolyn's whole body started to quiver. 'Don't say things like that!' she choked out.

'Why not? It's the truth. I want you so much that I can't think straight any more! My work is going to pot and so am I. I thought I could get over you. I thought it was just a matter of time. But then I saw you today and it all started up again. There's no escaping it. I can see that now. I want you. And do you know what else? You still want me too. I saw it today in your eyes, and I heard it tonight in your voice. You were jealous of Anthea, even though you have no reason to be. I haven't touched her since I met you.'

'I don't believe you.'

'I don't blame you. That's why I want to talk to you first, to apologise for all those rotten things I said, and to show you how much I still want you.'

Carolyn tried not to let his words excite her; tried not to start thinking about what it would feel like to hold him in her arms again.

'You... you keep away from me,' she cried out.

'Not in a month of Sundays! I'm coming over and I'm coming over *now*!'

She shook her head in silent despair, for the temptation to surrender herself once more was incredibly strong.

'No, Vaughan. Please don't. I . . . I won't let you in!' she finished wildly.

'I don't think you understand who you're dealing with here, Carolyn,' he countered fiercely. 'I can be very single-minded when I want to be. I want you and you want me. We're right for each other. I'm not going to let anything stand in the way of our being together, certainly not your misplaced and over-protective concern for your mother!'

He laughed, a scornful and frustrated sound. 'Oh, yes, I understand full well what's at the basis of your rejecting me. But it's high time for you to really grow up, my darling. Life's full of mistakes and regrets, but one doesn't compound them by letting them affect the rest of their lives. You face them, then get up and go on. You don't draw back and hide. There are no safe paths in life, Carolyn. It's packed with more risks and dangers and chances than those boys took that night down at the rock pool. For a while there, I did what you're doing. I turned my back on it like a bloody coward. But I'm getting back up on the wall now and facing those waves, no matter how large. I'm coming to get you, Carolyn. And *nothing* is going to stop me!'

CHAPTER ELEVEN

CAROLYN stared down at the dead receiver in her hands, Vaughan's amazing and passionate words echoing in her ears. Fifteen minutes, she calculated shakily. Twenty at most, for him to get from his house to this one.

She dropped the hand piece into its cradle and whirled round. Then stopped in her tracks. What could she do? Where could she go?

'To Maddie's!' she decided aloud and, holding up her ankle-length nightie, began to run towards the staircase, long blonde hair flying out behind. I must hurry, she urged herself. Get dressed. Find the keys. Lock up. Then off to Maddie's before Vaughan arrives!

Carolyn ground to a halt at the head of the stairs. No! Not Maddie's. That was the first place Vaughan would look for her when he found this place deserted. Besides, Maddie was not to be trusted in this. She had already given Vaughan her phone number, probably in some misguided attempt to manoeuvre them back together again. The woman had no conception of normal moral standards. Her rule in life seemed to be, man wants woman, then man *has* woman. And vice versa.

Carolyn groaned. She had nowhere else to go really. To drive around aimlessly was a stupid idea. *And* dangerous, since she'd been drinking.

Which was another reason why she couldn't face Vaughan tonight. She felt too vulnerable, too...weak. Tomorrow, she could call him at his office, offer to meet him somewhere publicly where she could talk to him again and try to explain why she couldn't have an affair with him. She would tell him that it wasn't a matter of taking risks. It was a matter of right and wrong, of living with one's conscience, of not selfishly grabbing happiness for oneself at the expense of another's.

Uncertainty gripped at her insides. Somehow she didn't think Vaughan would be a reasonable listener on this subject. He'd been so vehement over the phone. So *intense*! She'd heard of men becoming sexually obsessed with a woman, but she'd never envisaged herself being the object of such an obsession.

Against all common sense, she found the idea of Vaughan's being unable to control his passion unbearably exciting. In fact, she was appalled to find that her nipples had hardened at the thought. At the same time she couldn't stop thinking about how determined he'd sounded; couldn't stop thinking about what he might do to her, if she let him in.

'I can't!' she moaned aloud. Then steeled herself. 'I won't!'

She turned and raced, not down the stairs to the bedrooms, but up the other one to check that all the security deadlocks on the main doors had been turned.

They had.

She breathed a ragged sigh of relief. Vaughan had made the two lower floors of this house virtually impregnable. An intruder would need a battering ram to get through the heavy double doors that formed the only entry from outside.

Carolyn returned to the living-room still wringing her hands. No matter what logic she used, she still didn't feel safe. She wondered what time it was, and how long it had been since Vaughan had rung. Her watch was in one of the downstairs bathrooms, and there wasn't a clock around on this floor. She would have to mention that to Maddie, came the rather incongruous thought. No clocks in the living-rooms.

A flash of inspiration reminded her of the clock built into the wall oven. She hurried across the apricot-carpeted area into the black slate-floored kitchen and saw that it was seven-twenty. Not that that told her how long since Vaughan had rung, her ears straining for the sound of the MG pulling into one of the carports overhead.

A waste of time, she finally realised. The cement floors were thick, the whole place reinforced for peace and privacy. One couldn't even hear the semi-trailers rattling along the highway which was not all that far away.

Carolyn's tension became acute. She paced up and down the large galley-style kitchen for a while, then returned to the living-room. She sat down on the sofa's edge and pretended to watch the game show that was just finishing. But every nerve-ending in her body was stretched tight, waiting for Vaughan's furious demand that she let him in.

But the one problem that tormented her the most was...would she have the strength to turn him away?

Picking up the remote control for the TV she changed the channel to a current affairs programme. Taking a deep steadying breath she was about to settle back when a sudden crashing sound behind her sent her jumping to her feet, blue eyes round with shock as she whirled to face the balcony.

'Oh, my God!' she gasped in disbelief.

For it seemed that her very determined admirer had somehow scaled down from the floor above via a rope. Which was almost an impossibility, since the top floor jutted out over the balcony below like an overhanging roof. There was no way of reaching the lower floor at all by rope, unless one swung out over the sheer drop of the valley below then back in over the parapet to safety. Which is what Vaughan must have done, collecting an outdoor chair as he crashed-landed on to the veranda.

She stared, goggle-eyed, as he picked himself up, righted the chair and walked in through the open glass doors. 'I see I have some way to go before I become James Bond,' he remarked drily, dusting himself off and tucking his shirt back into the waistband of his trousers.

Yet James Bond was *exactly* what Carolyn thought he looked like, carrying off such an energetic and dangerous entry with all the dash and suaveness of the super secret agent. He rather *looked* like a James Bond too, still wearing the impeccable navy suit Carolyn had seen on him that afternoon, only the tie having been discarded. The rest of him was equally impeccable, the acrobatics not having disturbed a single hair of his short chestnut-brown hair.

Glittering dark eyes roved down over the slender length of her, barefoot and obviously naked under the clinging blue nightie. Her breathing grew shallow when his gaze lingered on her breasts, their high, lush outline hardly hidden by the thin silky material, or the way the neckline scooped low beneath shoestring straps. Carolyn grew hotly aware of their swelling under his scrutiny, their peaks pointy and hard. They tormented her with their arousal, mocking her earlier resolve to resist him.

It's no use, she realised in despair. If he touches me, I'm done for!

When he came closer, his eyes having narrowed with both intent and desire, she stayed stock-still, her breathing suspended, her eyes dilated with expectant fear.

'So glad to see you've dressed for the occasion,' he drawled, one hand snaking out to curl around her waist. Ever so slowly he drew her hard against him.

She said nothing, her throat suddenly raw, her head automatically tipping back in unspoken readiness for him. He was going to kiss her. And she was utterly incapable of stopping him.

But he didn't kiss her. At least...not at that precise moment. Instead he bent to slide his other arm around her thighs and hoisted her up into his arms. Then, he kissed her.

'Admit you still want me,' he rasped after his hungry mouth finally lifted from hers.

'I...I...'

'Never mind. Your body's already told me all I need to know.' He began walking, carrying her with ease. 'It's perfectly all right,' he went on, smiling wryly down at her tongue-tied and dazed self. 'You don't have to give me directions. I know the way to the bedrooms. I put them there.'

She gulped and closed her eyes as he made his way steadily down the wide carpeted stairs into the cool dimness of the passageway below. Her heart was going like a thrashing machine, her mind and emotions in chaos.

'By the way,' he grated out when he stopped to kick the main guest-room door open, 'it came to me as I was swinging through space a minute ago, with the possibility of certain death if I slipped, that I hadn't made one thing clear to you.'

She fluttered bewildered lashes open and looked up. His eyes locked with hers, startling her with their smouldering intensity.

'I love you,' he said, and strode purposefully into the room.

Carolyn woke to the confusion of Vaughan making love to her yet again. His long lean fingers moved between her thighs, reawakening her desire with his expertly knowing touch.

'No,' she protested weakly. 'Please...'

He totally ignored her, continuing till the movements of her hips told him she was ready. Covering her quickly, he drove his own formidably re-aroused flesh deep into her body.

A moaning, responsive shudder ran through her, and soon she was drowning in the heavy sensuality of Vaughan's lovemaking. When he stopped abruptly, she whimpered, glazed eyes flying open to stare up at his strained face.

'Tell me you love me too,' he urged. 'I want to hear you say it.'

Her heart leapt, but instinct warned her not to admit to such a thing. 'No,' she panted. 'No...'

He muttered something and resumed his slow, steady rhythm, taking her inexorably towards the moment when will-power would cease to exist, when there was nothing but her body and his, teetering on the brink of ecstasy.

At this most crucial moment, Vaughan stopped once again, bringing a cry of sharp need from her gasping lungs. Her nails dug deeply in his back and her body urged him desperately to continue.

'Tell me you love me, dammit,' he demanded, holding her still beneath him in an iron grip.

She whipped her head from side to side till he captured her mouth with his own, grinding her head back into the soft pillow with a savage kiss.

'Say it!' he gasped when his mouth finally burst from hers. 'Dear God, just say it this once!'

She was moved, more by the desperate note in his voice than his violent kiss, or the sexual edge on which she was hanging.

'I love you,' she cried huskily. 'I've loved you all along.'

A deep groaning shudder reverberated through him, startling Carolyn with the realisation that his demand had not been a mere testing of his physical power over her, but a genuine and sincere need to hear her voice the depth of her feelings.

He really does love me, she finally accepted, though with a sense of incredulity.

But then Vaughan resumed making love to her, with a fierce ardour, and all talking and thought ceased. There was nothing but two people locked together in a mating so feverish and frantic that just to keep breathing was task enough. The air around them moved with their energy and heat, shook when they shook, fell silent when they fell silent. This was loving at its best—and worst. Primitive... passionate... painful and possessive.

Vaughan held her afterwards as though he couldn't bear to have her a hair's breadth from him till their bodies and breathing had returned to normal.

'We'll get married,' he said at last, their flesh still fused as one. 'As soon as possible.'

Carolyn's automatic thrill of joy was soon replaced by nagging doubts. How could she and Vaughan ever find a lasting happiness together? How could the problem of her mother ever be solved?

'God, I can read you like a book,' he sighed, staring down at her troubled face. 'It's Isabel again, isn't it?'

Carolyn could have cried. Already it was happening. Already the ghost of the past was coming between them.

'She can't possibly still be in love with me,' he muttered angrily. 'If she ever damned well was!'

'Believe me, Vaughan,' Carolyn said bleakly, 'she *was*.' Obviously he had no conception of his own sexual magnetism, of how he could bewitch a woman against her will. Neither did he appreciate how emotionally and mentally fragile Isabel had become. How could he? He'd only seen her as a strong, competent woman.

A black realisation twisted at Carolyn's insides. No, she accepted bleakly. That wasn't so. Vaughan had also seen Isabel McKensie as an aroused, passionate woman.

Carolyn bit her bottom lip in sudden torment. Much as she believed Vaughan truly loved her, she still wasn't convinced that he hadn't actually made love to her mother all those years ago. The relentless thought kept recurring that he must have done more than he'd admitted to, to make sense of her mother's breakdown.

She looked up at him, unable to hide the anguish in her eyes. Before she could say another word he abruptly withdrew and rolled away from her.

Carolyn was shattered at the ghastly emptiness she felt at his sudden severing of their union. It wasn't so much a physical emptiness, as an emotional one. Vaughan's exasperation with her had suddenly put a barrier between them, a barrier born of a totally different way of looking at the situation. He clearly believed there was no real problem, no impedient to their marriage. It was simply a matter of putting the past behind them.

But life wasn't as simple as that...

'If you think you're going to keep our relationship a secret then you can think again,' he ground out. 'I've done nothing I'm ashamed of with your mother, and I refuse to act as if I have. Julian is a man of the world and will understand perfectly what happened. Isabel will blush for five minutes then forget all about it. You are making a mountain out of a molehill, Carolyn. And I won't be any part of it. You are to tell them both the truth as soon as they come home. If you don't, then I will!'

When she said nothing he sat up abruptly and swung his legs over the side of the bed. 'I'm going to have a shower. By the time I get out I hope you'll have come to your senses!'

'Vaughan, wait!' she called after him. He stopped at the bathroom door and turned slowly to face her.

'Did...did you love your mother?' she asked shakily.

He glared at her for a long long moment. 'Yes,' he bit out. 'Very much.'

'And would you have knowingly and deliberately risked hurting her?'

He looked at her with eyes that knew exactly what she was doing. 'No, of course not,' he agreed on a frustrated note.

'One week,' she pleaded. 'Just give me one week after they get back before you make a re-appearance in Mum's life. She's not as strong as we are, Vaughan. I...I need time to prepare her. To...to smooth the way...'

His smile was rueful. 'That's hitting below the belt and you know it. But I suppose I could spare a week out of a lifetime.'

She sighed her relief.

'And when exactly are our happy honeymooners due to dock in Sydney?'

'Next Friday.'

'Only seven days away,' he said thoughtfully, his eyes dropping to the floor.

'Yes.' She sounded and felt suddenly depressed. Too soon, she thought. Much too soon. They'd only just found each other.

He looked up, and a wicked grin split his face. 'There's one really positive and uplifting thought about seven days.'

'Oh? What?'

'Seven days have seven nights!'

CHAPTER TWELVE

'MUM! Julian! Over here!'

Carolyn waved madly, some of the tension that had been building up in her all morning lessening at the sight of her mother, beaming at her through the crowd. If Julian had already mentioned Vaughan's name, there was sure to have been some sign on her mother's face.

'Carolyn! Darling!' Isabel dropped her luggage and raced forward, literally throwing herself into her daughter's arms. 'Oh, I've missed you so,' she said, pulling back to cup Carolyn's face and kiss her in typical European fashion, on both cheeks.

'My, what a welcome!' Carolyn returned with some amazement. 'And how gorgeous you look. All sleek and tanned. And that *has* to be a Paris original you're wearing,' she admired, looking over her mother's slender figure encased in a stylish dress of emerald-green linen. 'Julian, you've been spoiling my mother outrageously,' she added as her stepfather joined them, loaded up to the hilt.

'Guilty as charged,' he grinned.

'You've been ages in Customs.'

Julian rolled his eyes. 'Your mother went overboard on presents for you, most of which we had to declare.'

Carolyn smiled at her mother. 'You naughty lady! But I won't say no. I just *adore* presents. Here, Julian, let me help you.'

'Me too, dear,' Isabel offered with a bouncy en-
thusiasm that momentarily startled Carolyn. She
stared for a second as her mother sparred playfully
with Julian over just what she could carry.

'You can have this one,' he teased, handing her
the largest suitcase. 'It contains her perfume pur-
chases,' he told Carolyn with mock dryness.

'He's exaggerating,' Isabel laughed.

'Don't you believe it!'

Carolyn could hardly contain her relief and joy.
They were both so relaxed and happy with each
other. And her *mother*! She was a different woman
from the uncertain, timid creature she'd seen off a
couple of months ago. Why, she was almost her old
confident self. Perhaps Vaughan was right. Perhaps
the past wouldn't be such a big problem after all.

Thinking about Vaughan brought a resurgence
of nerves. He had insisted that she make no attempt to keep his identity a secret. There was to be
no pulling Julian to one side. No lying. Isabel was
to be openly told who the architect who'd designed
her new home was.

And Carolyn had given her word.

Nevertheless, she hoped to break the news with
a gentle nonchalance that would reduce the possibility of her mother being too shocked. Preferably,
not in Julian's company.

The three of them shared out the luggage and
started to make their way through the busy terminal. The strain of hoping her stepfather wouldn't
let the cat out of the bag prematurely had Carolyn
chattering away.

'You'll be pleased to know that your lovely car
is in one piece, Julian. Not a dent in sight. In fact

I became so spoiled driving it around that I got rid of my old Datsun. I'm going to go out next week and look for something a bit more reliable.'

A light drizzle was falling when they emerged from the terminal, but it wasn't heavy enough to do much damage in the couple of minutes it took them to reach the car park and the BMW. They bundled most of the cases in the boot and the rest on the front passenger seat. Julian and Isabel seemed quite happy to sit like lovebirds in the back while Carolyn acted as chauffeur.

'Where to?' she asked her stepfather. 'Straight to Wollongong? Or do you want to stop off at your place here in Sydney first?' Julian was a widower of five years whose only child—a son—had moved to New Zealand not long after his mother's death. After living in a huge house down on the south coast all alone for a couple of years, he'd sold it and moved into a penthouse unit in Sydney, where he'd been equally lonely till he'd met Isabel.

'Straight to Wollongong for now,' he replied. 'I have plenty of clothes with me. What about you, Isabel? Do you need to go to your flat at Ashfield first?'

'Can't,' Carolyn intervened, glancing in the rear-view mirror at their puzzled faces. 'I vacated last week. Moved all the stuff we might need down to the house. Sold everything we didn't. Hope you don't mind, Mum, but I even got rid of that ghastly sideboard.'

'No, I don't mind,' said an amazed Isabel. 'Not at all. But goodness, wasn't that a lot of work for you?'

'I had plenty of time on my hands once I quit my job.'

Isabel frowned. 'But wouldn't you have had to work out your notice? Are you saying you just walked out?'

The reproach in her mother's voice was only to be expected. She was a real stickler for 'doing the right thing'.

'I—er—was having a bit of a problem with one of the doctors and thought it best to leave straight away.'

'What do you mean?' Isabel asked. 'What sort of problem?'

'She means sexual harassment,' Julian explained. 'Every working girl comes across it sooner or later. At least, every girl does,' he added drily, 'who looks like Carolyn. Which reminds me...that architect of mine hasn't been bothering you, has he?'

Oh, God...I just knew this was going to happen, Carolyn groaned, though colouring fiercely at the memory of the various ways Julian's architect had 'bothered' her this last week. Vaughan had refused to let her leave his side. They slept together, ate together, showered together. He even took her to work with him so that every spare moment he could whisk her off somewhere, either to his house or the beach or to some private and romantic spot where they could be alone. If anyone had asked her if it was possible to make love in a vintage MG, she would have laughed. Well ... she had incontrovertible proof that it was not only possible, but fantastic!

'Damn that man!' Julian grumbled, totally mis-interpreting her blush. 'Hell, I should have known better than to leave a girl as attractive as you in the clutches of a Casanova like that!'

'Julian! Carolyn! What are you two talking about? Julian, you never said anything at all to me about this! In fact, you didn't talk about the architect at all, except to say he was brilliant. Are you saying he's some sort of lecher and that Carolyn's been having to deal with him?'

Julian sighed and Carolyn gulped. Her hands tightened on the steering-wheel. It was difficult to concentrate on the traffic with her stomach churning and her eyes darting continuously to the mirror to see her mother's reactions.

'Something like that,' Julian muttered.

Carolyn gathered her wits and did her best to defuse the situation. 'Don't be silly, Julian. He's not like that at all. People get the wrong idea about him because he's single and handsome. Really, he was a perfect gentleman. And very easy to work with. Believe it or not, he turned out to be someone I already knew.'

She took a deep breath and hoped she'd gone some way to changing Julian's opinion of Vaughan's character before she went on. For the die had been cast. She had to reveal Vaughan's identity right here and now. But she had to act non-chalant... unconcerned... as though Vaughan was just an inconsequential name from the past. A coincidence.

After all, her mother had no idea Carolyn knew what she did about them, just as she had no idea what her mother's present feelings were for

Vaughan. All she could do was try to gauge Isabel's emotional state by her reaction to the news.

If not too bad, then after a while Vaughan and Carolyn could start openly going out together, as though their relationship had just begun. It wasn't the best of solutions, she conceded, but it was infinitely kinder than Vaughan's idea of just fronting up and telling Isabel about their relationship point-blank. Truly, the man had no sensitivity!

Yet in his dealings with his own family he had been quite wonderful, it seemed, having supported his widowed mother and five younger brothers and sisters ever since his father died some years ago in a mining accident at Broken Hill Mines.

Vaughan had confided quite a bit of his background during their long hours of being together this last week, and Carolyn had more than once felt guilty at how hastily she'd judged him in the past. The reason he'd always worked so obsessively and might have appeared somewhat penny-pinching was because most of his money had been channelled into giving the same college education to his siblings that his father had given him.

The last girl, Jesse, had just graduated from her nursing course last year so that the financial burden on Vaughan had finally been lifted. He'd already designed and had built for his mother a lovely home to replace the ancient monstrosity he'd been brought up in, and had booked her on a world cruise for this year when she'd been struck down by a fatal stroke.

Yes, he'd been a loving and generous son. Carolyn only hoped he would continue to understand her own wish to look after Isabel with the same consideration and devotion.

She glanced in the mirror at her mother's expectant face, and drummed up a carefree smile.

'Actually you know him too, Mum. It's Vaughan Slater. You remember? He boarded with us for a while ages and ages ago.'

All the blood drained from her mother's lovely face, making it look grey and pinched.

Carolyn swung her eyes back to the road as her whole stomach turned over.

'Vaughan...Slater?' Isabel repeated, obviously trying not to sound as shocked as she had looked.

'That's right.' Carolyn battled to keep up her unworried act but inside, she knew it was all going to be useless. Her relationship with Vaughan was not going to work. If the mere mention of his name could do this to her mother, then what would introducing him as her lover do?

'A boarder, did you say?' Julian joined in. 'Well, for heaven's sake, what a strange coincidence! But there again, they say fact is stranger than fiction. And you say he was a perfect gentleman? I *am* surprised. But pleased. I must call him when we get to the house and ask him over for a drink, thank him for everything. The telephone is connected, isn't it? I specifically asked for that to be done before I got back.'

'Yes. Everything's completely finished and fantastic,' Carolyn said, hoping against hope that her mother would gather her wits before Julian put two and two together and came up with four and a half. 'You'll be thrilled with it, I'm sure. Even the pool's full of water. As for the inside... Well... Maddie's been as efficient and brilliant as Vaughan.'

'*Maddie*?' Julian questioned. 'Oh, you mean Miss Powers? I'd forgotten her first name was Madeline.'

'Yes, we've become good mates. Oh, and you were wrong about her and Vaughan, Julian. They're definitely just good friends. In fact, they go a long way back. As for asking Vaughan over for a drink, I'm afraid that's not possible,' she went on, trundling out the excuse they'd prepared. 'He's interstate for a week. He said he'd ring you when he returns next Friday.'

Carolyn couldn't help but see her mother's intense relief. It made her want to cry.

'I see,' Julian said. 'Well you seem to have done splendidly, daughter, dear, overseeing everything and organising such a big move. I'm most grateful to you. And most pleased you've chucked in that dull job to live with us. Come next week, I'll ring up all my contacts down south and see what we can do about getting you an interesting position. Have you any idea what you'd like to do?'

Carolyn was grateful to talk about something else, other than Vaughan. Quite surreptitiously, she noticed that after a few minutes her mother's colour had returned, and, while she was sitting very still, Isabel was now hiding her distress surprisingly well. This in itself was a minor miracle. The Isabel of a few weeks ago wouldn't have been capable of masking her emotions so adeptly. She even finally joined into the conversation.

'Enough talk of jobs,' she said with a brightness that might have been forced, but didn't seem to be.

'I want to tell Carolyn about our trip. Remember how we used to think Europe was...'

The rest of the drive to Wollongong was taken up with a lively documentation of their travels, with Julian and Isabel often differing over what they liked most, though never with any rancour. A vague hope returned to Carolyn as she bore witness to this much more confident and assertive Isabel, so that by the time they arrived at the house she climbed out from behind the steering-wheel with some degree of optimism.

The house was as big a hit as she thought it would be.

'Oh, Julian!' Isabel exclaimed for the umpteenth time when they finally made it out on to the main balcony.

The dangling rope had thankfully long been removed, but Carolyn couldn't walk out there without thinking of Vaughan's crazily wonderful entrance, without her whole insides being warmed by the love they shared. She knew that she could never give him up. Never! But there again, she didn't want to hurt her mother either. Her dismay at being caught in such a dreadful dilemma was acute.

'I've never seen a view like this,' Isabel enthused. 'We've been halfway around the world and nothing compares. Oh, Julian, thank you...thank you...'

Carolyn was startled when her mother threw herself into her husband's arms and kissed him. For a few seconds they seemed oblivious to her presence. Julian eventually pulled back, clearing his throat awkwardly. Isabel's blush was a beautiful combination of embarrassment and heightened sensuality.

Well! Carolyn thought, surprised, but very very pleased. There was certainly nothing platonic about her mother and Julian any more. Obviously there was much to be said for a honeymoon cruise and six weeks in Europe!

'I tell you what we'll do,' Julian suggested with pride. 'We'll have a housewarming party and invite everyone we know. And we'll make it next weekend, so Vaughan'll be back in time. How about that?'

'Fine,' Isabel agreed, but Carolyn noted that at the mention of Vaughan she had quickly turned her face away and was even now walking over to the balcony wall. Her knuckles turned white as they curled around the circular tubing that ran a couple of inches above the top of the parapet.

Carolyn didn't know what to think any more.

If it had been her decision and hers alone, she would ask Vaughan not to come to that party, to give Isabel and Julian's marriage more time before he came back into Isabel's life.

But she knew Vaughan would not do that. By next Saturday night, their agreed week would be up, and wild horses wouldn't keep him away from Julian's housewarming.

Carolyn's heart sank. She wasn't looking forward to that party. She just knew it would end in disaster!

CHAPTER THIRTEEN

'I DON'T know what you're so worried about,' Vaughan said. 'From what you told me, your mother took the news quite well. Come back to bed, darling. We have another hour before I have to be at work.'

Carolyn stayed standing at the window for a few more seconds, Vaughan's bathrobe clutched tightly around her, forcing herself to exert some will-power and not run to him every time he wanted her. Already this past week she'd invented a whole host of excuses to leave the house so she could be alone with Vaughan. This morning she'd come up with an early hairdressing appointment, driving off before eight in the Corona she'd bought with her savings the previous weekend.

'I . . . I must be getting home, Vaughan,' she lied, her back to him. 'I have to help Mum with preparations for the party tonight.'

He said nothing and she could feel him staring at her across the room. She stayed stubbornly where she was, every silent second like an eternity. She was about to whirl round when his hands suddenly curved over her shoulders.

'Julian told me on the telephone that he'd hired caterers,' he said calmly. 'And the house could hardly be that dirty yet.'

Carolyn's whole insides quivered when he eased her back against his hard frame. God, was it always

going to be like this? she agonised.
Instantaneous ... explosive ...

Every muscle in her body tensed as she waited
for him to dip his head, to nuzzle her neck, to trail
wet kisses over her hot, hot skin. When his lips
finally contacted the fluttering pulse at the base of
her throat she moaned, twisting her neck around,
blindly seeking his mouth with her own. Vaughan
covered it with a raw groan, ripping the bathrobe
from her body while he drank from the sweetness.
Then, when she was once again naked and trembling in his arms, he lifted her and carried her
swiftly to the bed.

Carolyn was a hot-bed of nerves. It was nearly nine.
The house was filled with people. Yet Vaughan was
still to put in an appearance.

Maddie, who had finally recovered from the
shock of finding out Vaughan had actually fallen
in love and was talking marriage, was doing her
level best to soothe Carolyn with her original brand
of intuition and logic. 'You have nothing to worry
about, sweetie. I've been watching your mother and
Julian together and their body language speaks of
mutual adoration. Vaughan has long been forgotten, believe me.'

Carolyn could not agree. Maddie had not seen
her mother's initial reaction to the news about
Vaughan. And then there was the evidence of Isabel
not having mentioned his name all week. If he
meant nothing to her any more, then why not talk
about him? Even yesterday, when Julian had made
the telephone call to Vaughan's office to thank him
for the house and invite him to the party, Isabel

had been conspicuous in her quick exit from the room.

No... Maddie was wrong this time. Isabel was still harbouring feelings for Vaughan. Carolyn was sure of it.

The musical doorbell pealed once more over the noise of the subtle background music and chatting guests. Its ringing was like chalk scraping on a blackboard to Carolyn's nerves, for sooner or later it would be Vaughan behind the door, Vaughan confronting her mother again with all his mature magnetic beauty, Vaughan... the man Isabel had once loved madly, and who was now equally madly loved by her daughter.

Carolyn's apprehension increased as she saw Julian and Isabel hurry from the living-room in the direction of the front doors.

'God, Carolyn,' Maddie drawled, and took a swig of her martini, 'you look as if the doctor just told you you have twenty-four hours to live. Have some faith in your mum, will you? She's a very sensible woman. Not at all the way I pictured. And a real lady. There won't be any scenes or swoonings from her after she sees Vaughan again. She has a husband of her own now. She's not a vulnerable, single, sex-starved spinster any more.

'Speaking of sex-starved,' Maddie went on in a husky whisper, 'I've just seen a gorgeous specimen of manhood over in a corner who's looking awfully lonely. Can't have that, can I?' And she swanned off, a vibrant vampirish figure in flowing black chiffon and clouds of exotic perfume.

Carolyn had no time to feel remotely sorry for Maddie's next male victim. Her attention was riveted on the trio who'd just entered the living-room.

Her eyes flew first to her mother, svelte and stylish in peacock-blue silk and diamonds. Carolyn felt almost dowdy in her plain black dress and pearls. But behind her mother's sparkling elegance was undeniable stress, spelt out by the way Isabel's hands were clenched tightly at her sides.

And right next to her left side stood Vaughan, magnificent in casual cream trousers, and an open-necked brown shirt. Julian was beside him, smiling and saying something to Vaughan. But his wife wasn't smiling. She was frowning, and her eyes kept flicking sideways at Vaughan then away again, as though she couldn't bear to look at him for too long.

All Carolyn's fears were consolidated as she watched her mother's agitation, sending a black despair into her heart.

Suddenly, Vaughan looked across the room at her. He must have seen distress written on her face, for he quickly excused himself from his host and hostess and began walking towards her. Carolyn couldn't help but notice her mother's eyes follow his every move.

'I think you could do with a drink,' Vaughan said once he reached her. 'Come on...' He steered her over to the bar where he poured her a stiff Scotch from the decanters of the counter. 'Here...get that into you and start looking happy or your mother will wonder what's up.'

Carolyn gripped the glass in both hands and stared up at Vaughan. 'Happy? How can I look happy with disaster looming on the horizon?'

'What on earth are you talking out?' he retorted impatiently. 'Your mother's fine. Sure, she *was* a bit stiff with me, but that's only to be expected.'

'What did she say?'

'She thanked me politely for the house and said she was pleased to see I'd become as successful as she'd always thought I would be.'

'But didn't you see the way she *looked* at you?'

'She hardly looked at me at all! Good grief, Carolyn, why are you trying to make something out of nothing? Your mother is perfectly happy with Julian.'

'Oh, you men are so *blind*! Mum might have been happy with Julian, if you hadn't popped up again. But she isn't in love with Julian. She told me so. Other than my father, the only man she's ever loved is *you*!'

Vaughan's sigh was highly irritated. 'I've had about as much of this as I can take. The person who's blind is *you*. Isabel was *never* in love with me. I know that as surely as I know *I* love her crazy daughter. But you obviously need to hear it from the horse's mouth!'

Snatching the untouched glass of Scotch from her hands, he thumped it down on the bar and hauled her unceremoniously over to where Julian and Isabel were talking to Maddie and her latest prey.

'Do excuse me,' he interrupted bluntly, 'but Carolyn and I have a problem that only Isabel can solve. Do you think we could see you alone for a moment?' he asked the startled lady.

'Er—yes, of course.' She darted Carolyn a puzzled glance before turning to her husband.

'Julian? Will you look after our guests, see they all have drinks? That waiter we hired keeps getting lost. And Maddie . . . you keep Miles entertained for us.'

'My pleasure.' Maddie smiled gleefully.

Carolyn felt as if she was going to the guillotine as Vaughan pushed her after her mother's retreating figure.

'Well? How can I help you?' Isabel said once they reached the privacy of the study.

'There's no polite way to ask what I am about to ask, Isabel,' he began, and Carolyn groaned silently. 'I wouldn't ask at all except your daughter's happiness is at stake.'

Isabel looked alarmed. 'Carolyn's happiness?'

Carolyn shook her head in agitation.

'I need to know the reason behind your breakdown ten years ago.'

Isabel's gasp was followed by an anguished look in her daughter's direction. 'You told him about that? But *why*?'

Carolyn grimaced.

'Your daughter,' Vaughan interrupted swiftly, 'seems to have gained the impression that you were once in love with me. She was worried that my turning up in your life again might adversely affect your marriage. That's why she told me about your breakdown, to try to convince me to stay out of your life. I told her she was wrong to think I'd been the cause of your breakdown and that you had never loved me, but she just doesn't believe me.'

Isabel looked down at her suddenly twisting hands, a deep frown on her face. When she looked up again, her eyes carried fear. 'But what *made* you think I was in love with Vaughan?' she asked her daughter.

Carolyn had no option at this stage but to tell the truth. 'The day Vaughan left...I...I overheard you raving about how he'd told you he loved you, how you wouldn't have slept with him otherwise...'

Isabel looked appalled.

'I already suspected there was something between you,' Carolyn went on. 'You see, I...I saw you and Vaughan together the night before...in the living room. I'd come home early from ballet...'

Isabel's hands flew to clasp the sides of her face, pained eyes darting to Vaughan.

'Remember?' he said gently. 'I thought I heard a sound.'

The cheeks under her fingers went bright red. 'Oh, how awful... Oh, Carolyn... I'm so sorry... Oh, dear, I feel so ashamed...but...' her hands slipped back down to her sides and the expression in her eyes changed to a rueful regret '...you've got it all wrong.'

Carolyn's stomach flipped over. 'You mean you *didn't* love him?'

Her mother shook her head. 'No...I've only ever really loved one man in my whole life.'

Carolyn felt sick with relief. She turned to Vaughan. 'She's talking about my father.'

'No!' came her mother's startling denial. 'I don't mean your father. I'm talking about Julian.'

'But...but...'

Isabel came slowly forward and took her daughter's hands in hers. 'Carolyn...dear...I never wanted you to find out. I wanted you to keep believing that your father and mother had loved each other so much that their love transcended the rules of society.'

Carolyn was beyond words. She was stunned.

'I really thought I loved your father. But I was young, and easily impressed. And of course, he *said* he loved me. But his love was only lust and after a few months he didn't want me any more. The day he had his heart attack he'd just told me our love was a lie, that it was nothing but sex, that I bored the hell out of him and that he was going back to his wife. I was crushed ... mortified ... I'd broken all my moral rules for this man. I was having his baby in a couple of months and there he was telling me there had been nothing between us but sex.'

Isabel drew in a ragged sigh. 'Emotionally and mentally, I simply refused to accept such an un-romantic explanation for our actions. With his sudden death I was able to go on living the lie, convincing myself he *had* loved me. And that I had loved him. That lie became my strength, my motivation for going on alone. It wasn't until Vaughan came into my life that I finally understood the power of sexual frustration and need. I had been lonely for male company for some time. Then, suddenly, there was this gorgeous young man in my own home. I wouldn't have been human if I hadn't desired him under those circumstances. As the months went by I became more and more obsessed with having sex with him. Suddenly, the time drew near when he would be leaving. If I didn't act ...'

A guilty blush suffused her cheeks, but she kept her chin up bravely and Carolyn thought her mother had never been more wonderful. Or more courageous.

'I deliberately set out to seduce Vaughan the night you saw us together,' she confessed. 'I made him a fancy dinner, gave him wine, dressed seductively. I did everything I could to get him into bed with me. Of course, at the time I told myself I was in love with him. In my warped mind, sex and love had become inseparable. Vaughan wouldn't do it, however. He was worried about *you*. The next day, with the blunt honesty of youth, he made me see the truth for what it was. When I said I loved him, he forced me to see my lie and that I had acted solely from sexual need. Unfortunately, I had for far too long lived my life on the premise that this couldn't be so for a decent woman. When I was finally forced to face the fact that I hadn't loved your father any more than he had loved me I just couldn't cope. It was your father's treachery you heard me raving about that day. Not Vaughan's. Vaughan never did anything dishonourable at all.'

'I wouldn't say that,' Vaughan groaned. 'Indirectly, I *did* cause your breakdown, with my lack of tact. My insensitivity. Oh, Isabel, I'm so sorry...'

'Don't be,' Isabel said with a catch in her throat. 'You were young. And you only spoke the truth. You weren't to know you were dealing with such a weak woman.'

'Not weak, Isabel. Just sweet and kind and good. I would envy Julian,' he went on, drawing Carolyn close to his side, 'if I hadn't already captured for myself the heart of your lovely daughter.'

Isabel's beautiful blue eyes opened with astonishment as they moved from Carolyn to Vaughan
to Carolyn again.

'So,' she sighed, and dashed a tear from her eye.
'You've finally fallen in love.'

'Yes, Mum,' Carolyn admitted, her own eyes
shimmering.

'How wonderful... And you'll be getting
married?' she directed at Vaughan with a sterner
tone.

He grinned. 'As soon as possible.'

Isabel was slightly taken aback. 'You don't
mean...'

'No.' He laughed. 'I *don't* mean.'

'Not that it would matter,' Isabel relented, 'since
you're really in love.' She beamed at Carolyn. 'Well,
isn't this marvellous? And there I'd been, worried
stiff all week that Vaughan might say something in
front of you, and I'd lose your respect and love.'

Carolyn stepped forward and gave her mother a
hug. 'You could never do that, Mum.'

'That's just what Julian said.' Isabel wiped
another tear from her eye. 'I told him, of course,
what had happened all those years ago and he said
I was a silly goose to worry about what was a piece
of ancient history, and that even if I'd committed
high treason my darling daughter would still love
me. Oh he's such a wonderful man, Carolyn. I don't
know why it took me so long to realise how much
I loved him. Shall we go and tell him the good
news?'

'Why don't we tell everyone?' Vaughan suggested. 'What do you say, sweetheart?' And he gave

Carolyn a kiss on the cheek. 'Shall we announce our engagement tonight?'

She gazed up at him and tried awfully hard not to cry. 'We haven't a ring,' she choked out.

'Well, it just so happens...'

Carolyn stared as he drew a red velvet box from his pocket and flipped it open to reveal the most exquisite diamond. 'Shall we see if it fits?' he murmured.

Carolyn suddenly remembered Maddie making her try on a large ruby ring during the week, supposedly so she could look at it from a distance. 'Something tells me,' she said, a lump in her throat, 'that it'll be perfect.'

'Like the lady who will wear it,' he returned softly, and slipped it on to her finger.

Maddie sighed with exasperation as she watched the happy couple accepting kisses and congratulations from all and sundry. Truly, anyone would think that marriage was the be-all and end-all! Heavens, she would rather go to the dentist every day than get married. Horrid, boring institution!

When the throng around Vaughan and Carolyn lessened she sashayed forward and extended a scarlet-nailed hand to each of them. 'Best of luck, my darlings,' she said, thinking to herself that one would need a hell of a lot of luck to make a go of such an unnatural arrangement. Fancy expecting a woman to tie herself to one man for the rest of her life. Ridiculous!

'So tell me,' she drawled indulgently, 'what would you like for a wedding present? Ah, yes, I've just the thing. My services free to decorate that ghastly dump you live in, Vaughan. I'll enjoy making it habitable for your beautiful bride.' She smiled smugly at them. 'And I have just the painting to put over the fireplace!'

'No, you don't, Maddie, dear,' Vaughan vetoed. 'The only place that particular painting is going will be where no other male will ever see it and where it will do the most good. Over *my* bed!'

'What a party-pooper you are, Vaughan,' Maddie complained.

'Always have been,' he agreed with a grin, then leant close to whisper something in Carolyn's ear. She laughed and soon they were making a hurried exit.

'Where are Vaughan and Carolyn off to?' Julian asked Maddie.

'I think,' she said with a straight face, 'they have an urgent need to inspect the location for a painting I just gave them. Which reminds me...tell me about Miles, will you, Julian? I mean...he's not *married*, is he?'

'Let your hair down,' Vaughan said with seduction in his voice and desire in his glance.

'You keep your eyes on the road, you naughty man,' Carolyn reprimanded, though she did as he asked, unwinding her plait and fluffing her long hair out with her fingers. It blew out behind her as the MG whizzed along, making her feel free and invigorated and just a little bit wild.

'God, but I'm happy,' she cried, tipping back her head and laughing with the uninhibited joy of a person from whose shoulders an intolerable burden had just been lifted. Her mother didn't love

Vaughan; had *never* loved Vaughan. It was like a miracle come true.

She lifted her left hand and twisted it this way and that, the diamond ring flashing its brilliance under the street-lights.

'Like it?' Vaughan asked.

Her smile was slightly reproachful. 'Silly question.'

'Let's not wait long to be married, my darling.'

'No, let's not.'

Vaughan gave a low laugh. 'Just as well you aren't pregnant, though. I think Isabel would have skinned me alive if you were.'

'She wouldn't have minded, really. Neither would I. I'd love to have your baby, Vaughan. Not just one, either. I've always hated being an only child.'

Her heart turned over at the look he slid her way. It was full of love and wonder and admiration.

'You can have as many babies as you like, but do you honestly think I'd make a good father?'

'You'd be hopeless at first,' she teased. 'But given time . . . and practice . . .'

'How much practice?'

'Shall we say . . . half a dozen?'

'My God, if that's the number we're aiming for, we haven't a second to lose.'

It was probably coincidence that this was the precise moment they arrived at Vaughan's house, even though the MG *was* directed into the driveway with what Carolyn considered undignified haste.

'On second thoughts,' Vaughan went on as he snapped off the engine and hurdled over his door, 'I think that I should practise my fathering technique a little longer before we put it to the supreme test.'

'Do you, indeed?' Carolyn adopted a straight face before he reached her side of the car. 'I would have thought you'd auditioned quite well for the part already.' She had trouble stifling her giggles as she put her hand in his and allowed him to pull her to her feet and into his arms. 'Still, I *do* have this pathetically short memory span, and since it is already many hours since I sampled your...um...paternity potential, perhaps you should give me a further sample of your services before a firm decision is made?'

'Well! I've never heard such a disgracefully disguised sexual proposition in all my life!' he pronounced with mock disapproval. 'And to think it came from the sweet lips of the girl I love, the girl whose very innocence first captured my attention, who, might I add, constantly castigated me for my loose lifestyle, who——'

'Why don't you shut up and make love to me, you fool?' she rasped, and slid her arms up around his neck.

A satisfied smile pulled at his mouth as it swooped, leaving time for only two short words before it covered hers.

'Good idea.'

Next Month's Romances

Each month you can choose from a wide variety of romance with Mills & Boon. Below are the new titles to look out for next month, why not ask either Mills & Boon Reader Service or your Newsagent to reserve you a copy of the titles you want to buy — just tick the titles you would like and either post to Reader Service or take it to any Newsagent and ask them to order your books.

Please save me the following titles:		Please tick	√
BACHELOR AT HEART	Roberta Leigh		
TIDEWATER SEDUCTION	Anne Mather		
SECRET ADMIRER	Susan Napier		
THE QUIET PROFESSOR	Betty Neels		
ONE-NIGHT STAND	Sandra Field		
THE BRUGES ENGAGEMENT	Madeleine Ker		
AND THEN CAME MORNING	Daphne Clair		
AFTER ALL THIS TIME	Vanessa Grant		
CONFRONTATION	Sarah Holland		
DANGEROUS INHERITANCE	Stephanie Howard		
A MAN FOR CHRISTMAS	Annabel Murray		
DESTINED TO LOVE	Jennifer Taylor		
AN IMAGE OF YOU	Liz Fielding		
TIDES OF PASSION	Sally Heywood		
DEVIL'S DREAM	Nicola West		
HERE COMES TROUBLE	Debbie Macomber		

If you would like to order these books in addition to your regular subscription from Mills & Boon Reader Service please send £1.70 per title to: Mills & Boon Reader Service, P.O. Box 236, Croydon, Surrey, CR9 3RU, quote your Subscriber No:...
(If applicable) and complete the name and address details below. Alternatively, these books are available from many local Newsagents including W.H.Smith, J.Menzies, Martins and other paperback stockists from 4th December 1992.

Name:..

Address:..

....Post Code:........................

To Retailer: If you would like to stock M&B books please contact your regular book/magazine wholesaler for details.

You may be mailed with offers from other reputable companies as a result of this application.
If you would rather not take advantage of these opportunities please tick box ☐